Nelly the MONSTER Sitter

What they say about Nelly the Monster Sitter:

'Once I had started this book I didn't want to leave it.' Becky, age 11

'I would give this book 10 out of 10!' Suzi, age 8

'Nelly's adventures make you laugh and her ways of coping with the monster are very funny.' Niamh, age 10

'I enjoyed it so much I have passed it on to my friend . . . the funny monster names made me laugh out loud.' Alice, age 9

'It had me laughing from start to finish.' Katie, age 9

**Have you read the other
Nelly the Monster Sitter adventures?**

*You don't have to read these books in order,
but if you'd like to this is the order
that we recommend:*

1. Grerks, Squurms & Water Greeps
2. Cowcumbers, Pipplewaks & Altigators
3. Huffaluks, Muggots & Thermitts
4. Polabores, Digdiggs & Dendrilegs
5. Ultravores, Rimes & Wattwatts

Nelly the MONSTER Sitter

Polarbores, Digdiggs & Dendrilegs

KES GRAY

Illustrated by Stephen Hanson

Hodder
Children's
Books

A division of Hachette Children's Books

To the Pennicks at number eighteen

First published in Great Britain in 2007
by Hodder Children's Books

A Catalogue record for this book is available from the British Library

ISBN-13: 978 0 340 93191 2

Typeset in NewBaskerville by Avon DataSet Ltd,
Bidford on Avon, Warwickshire

Printed and bound in Great Britain by
Bookmarque Ltd, Croydon, Surrey

The paper and board used in this paperback by Hodder Children's
Books are natural recyclable products made from wood grown in
sustainable forests. The manufacturing processes conform to the
environmental regulations of the country of origin.

Hodder Children's Books
a division of Hachette Children's Books
338 Euston Road, London NW1 3BH
An Hachette UK company
www.hachette.co.uk

NELLY THE MONSTER SITTER

'If monsters are real, how come I've never seen one?' said Nelly.

'Because they never go out,' said her dad.

'Why don't monsters ever go out?' said Nelly.

'Because they can never get a baby sitter,' said her dad.

Nelly thought about it. Her mum and dad never went out unless they could get a baby sitter. Why should monsters be any different?

'Then I shall become Nelly the Monster Sitter!' smiled Nelly.

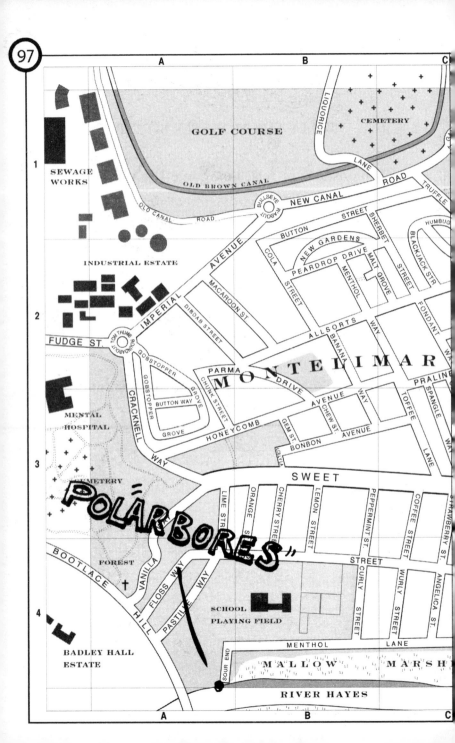

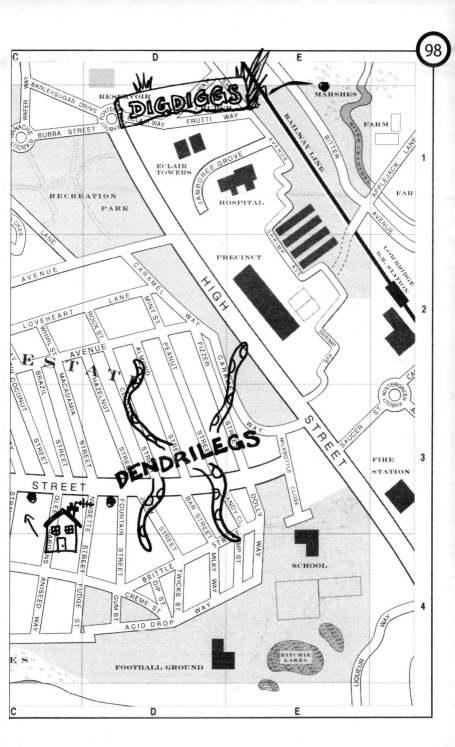

1

What is it with Sundays? Before you know it, the Sun is gone, the day's gone and your school homework deadlines are looming.

'Mu-um,' groaned Asti, from the desk in her bedroom, 'what were the biggest dinosaurs?'

'Ask Nelly,' shouted her mum, slipping an armful of autumn clothes from the coat hangers in her wardrobe and folding them neatly into a pile on her bed. 'She's the monster expert in this house.'

'Daaaaad!' shouted Asti, determined not to ask Nelly for anything. 'Who were the biggest dinosaurs around?'

'Tyrannosaurus Rexes, I think,' hollered her dad, lowering his foot from the loft hatch and gingerly feeling around for the top rung of the loft ladder.

'Argentinosaurus,' said Nelly, firing the correct answer through the crack of her bedroom door. 'Seismosaurus was the longest, but Argentinosaurus was the biggest.'

Asti shrugged her shoulders and stared glumly at her exercise book. The blank page before her was crowned with the spectacularly boring headline *Dinosaurs. Heroes to Zeros. Explain.*

She dragged her biro like a tree trunk to the top left-hand corner of the page and then groaned again. She hated writing essays, especially essays about subjects she hated writing essays about, i.e. any subject.

'Argentinosaurus was 110 feet long and weighed 100 tons; that's the same as twenty bull elephants,' shouted Nelly. 'They were twice as long as T Rexes.'

'Whoopdedoo!' Asti muttered.

'The biggest monkey dinosaur was definitely King Kong,' shouted her dad, tugging a bin bag full of old clothes down from the lip of the loft hatch and then jumping clear from the final three steps as it avalanched towards his head.

4

'Missed!' he smiled, as the bin bag fell on to the landing carpet with a squish and a clomp.

'King Kong, the amazing gorillasaurus. I saw him wrestling a T Rex on telly once. He must have eaten bananas the size of canoes!'

'King Kong wasn't real,' shouted Asti. 'He was a movie monster.'

'Well, I never knew that!' sighed her dad, slapping his forehead ironically and lifting the bin bag from the carpet. 'And there's me thinking a caveman had filmed the whole thing!'

'They didn't have gorillas in dinosaur times,' said Asti, grinding the nib of her biro into her rubber to see if she could push it all the way through. 'Or film cameras.'

'Or giant bananas!' laughed Nelly, nailing her dad's theory conclusively.

Nelly's dad conceded defeat. 'Well, you make sure you put that in your homework essays, girls,' he smiled. 'I'm sure I'm not alone in thinking that once upon a time, hairy gorillas the size of office blocks walked the earth with beautiful blondes tenderly clenched between the big fat furry fingers of one hand and giant bananas in the other.'

Asti lifted her biro again, but then sagged under the sheer weight of ink.

'Clifford, I need that bag of winter clothes,' shouted Mum. 'Can you stop talking about giant bananas and office blocks and help me sort my autumn collection out?'

'Gigantosaurus was the biggest meat eater,' shouted Nelly. She had finished her essay and was now relaxing on her bed, a mine of dinosaur information. 'Argentinosaurus probably looked scary, but it didn't eat meat.'

'Bit like your mum then,' laughed her dad, poking his head into Nelly's bedroom and plucking a green scarf from the bin bag.

'I heard that!' growled Nelly's mum from a forest of coat hangers.

Nelly looked up from her bed and smiled. Her dad had wrapped her mum's green silk scarf around his face and was baring his teeth at her like a velociraptor.

'What are you doing?' he asked, switching to

Dad mode again.

'Waiting for my monster sitting phone to ring,' Nelly replied.

'Are you expecting a call?' asked her dad.

'Not really,' said Nelly, 'but I've got a hunch I'm going to get one.'

'I've got a hunch your mum isn't going to want to wear any of last year's winter clothes this winter,' sighed her dad, unwinding the green silk scarf from his head and slipping it back into the bin bag.

'Me too,' smiled Nelly, putting her hands behind her head and easing back on to her pillow.

'Clothes bag PLEASE, Clifford!' boomed Nelly's mum from the wardrobe.

Nelly's dad slipped from view, and then reappeared unexpectedly.

'Have you done all your homework?' he asked hopefully.

Nelly nodded triumphantly.

'Then could you help Asti with hers, please?' asked her dad.

Nelly stiffened. Help Asti? Help lizard-faced,

poison-tongued Asti? WITH HER HOMEWORK?
No way! She'd rather help an Argentinosaurus
wipe its bottom.

Nelly's dad hovered by the bedroom door and
fixed her with pleading adult eyes.

Nelly wedged her shoulders firmly into her
pillow and glared back with immovable monster
sitter eyes.

'No more lifts,' said her dad, pulling his car
keys from his pocket and dangling them like a
bunch of mini carrots.

'Oh . . . OK . . .' grimaced Nelly.

2

By the time Nelly had arrived at her sister's bedroom door, she had engineered a plan. OK, it wasn't a great plan, but at least it was plan enough to make the chore of helping Asti bearable.

She knocked lightly and waited for an icy blast to whistle from the direction of Asti's homework desk.

'Who is it?' snapped Asti, like a troll with a toothache.

'Me,' said Nelly, bristling at the prospect of having to enter her sister's room.

'Bog off, Me!' snapped Asti.

Nelly turned to go, then checked herself with the thought of no more monster sitting lifts.

'Let me in,' she said, turning to face the door again. 'I've got something for you.'

Asti pulled the nib of her biro out of her pencil

rubber and stabbed it into the surface of her desk.

'What is it?' she asked.

'My dinosaur essay,' said Nelly. 'If you want, I'll let you have a read.'

Asti turned stiffer than a fossil. The voice at the door certainly sounded like her sister, but its words sounded nothing like Nelly at all.

'If you have a read of my essay, it might help you write yours,' said Nelly, almost choking on the niceness of what she was saying. 'You can copy it if you like.'

A pause ensued on both sides of the door.

Asti sat bolt upright in her chair, staring down at the word *Zero* in her homework title. Zero was all that she had written.

Nelly stood, shoulders slumped, wondering how many years of psychiatric counselling she was going to need after spending more than a nanosecond in Asti's bedroom.

A pause followed the pause, and then another five pauses popped up silently between the seven more pauses that came after that.

'The door's open,' blurted Asti, eventually unable to resist the opportunity to get her homework done the simple pimple way.

Nelly sighed, placed her hand on the white porcelain door knob, and braced herself for the colour pink.

There was lots of pink in Asti's bedroom. A month ago there had been lots of lilac, but pink was her newest favourite colour. Asti changed favourite colours like some boys at school changed football teams; however, for the brief period that she supported a colour, she supported it big time. Her wallpaper was pink, her ceiling was pink, her lampshade was pink, her bed quilt was pink, her pillow cases were pink, the pencil case on her homework desk was pink and her carpet was lilac (but due to be changed).

Nelly stepped reluctantly into the room and closed the door behind her. It was like walking into a poodle parlour.

'Where is it then?' yapped Asti, scanning her sister like a supermarket barcode for signs of a dinosaur essay. Nelly pulled four sheets of neatly written A4 paper out from under her jumper and wafted them seductively in the air.

'Not a word to Mum or Dad,' she whispered. 'Dad would go up the wall if he knew I was helping you.'

Asti's eyes flashed to the bedroom door and then back to Nelly. 'Why are you doing this?' she asked suspiciously.

'Doing what?' said Nelly innocently.

'This,' said Asti, pointing to the essay Nelly was holding.

'I just thought you might want some help, that's all,' fibbed Nelly. 'Monsters are totally not your thing, but they are totally mine, so I totally thought I'd do you a favour. Still, if you don't want my help, fine,' she huffed, turning back towards the bedroom door and feigning to leave.

Asti jumped from her seat and flagged Nelly down with both arms.

'Don't go,' she panicked. 'It's just that, well, you never help me do anything.'

'You never help me do anything either,' countered Nelly.

'So why are you helping me now?' pressed Asti.

Nelly approached Asti's homework desk with the look of a spy about to deliver a document of international importance. It was time to execute her plan.

'Because the way I figure it,' she said in hushed tones, 'if I do this for you, then there's no reason at all why you shouldn't do something for me.'

Asti shifted uncomfortably in her seat, one eye on the essay, the other on the essay.

'How do you mean?' she murmured.

'I mean, Sis,' said Nelly, stroking her essay like a Persian cat, 'that if I do this for you, then it would only be fair if the two of us came to a little arrangement.'

'What kind of arrangement?' frowned Asti.

'You pay me,' said Nelly with a mercenary smile. 'If you want to benefit from all my hard work and copy my essay then you can pay me.'

Asti's brain split like a tree trunk, falling in two very different directions at once. One side landed on the protest side; after all, the very thought of paying her sister so much as a penny turned her blood colder than glacial meltwater. The other side landed on the *however, if I can copy Nelly's essay, I'll have it done in two ticks, plus I'll get an A grade, plus I won't have to waste any more of my Sunday writing stupid essays, plus I'll be able spend some quality time persuading Mum that I need some new winter clothes too* side.

'How much?' said Asti.

'Five pounds,' said Nelly boldly.

'FIVE POUNDS!' squawked Asti, driving the nib of her biro deep into the grain of her desk. 'Where am I going to get five pounds?'

'Somewhere pink, I expect,' said Nelly, throwing a contemptuous glance around her sister's room.

Asti's face darkened, and then pinched with panic as Nelly turned towards the door and made to leave.

'Suit yourself,' said Nelly with a shrug.

Asti sprang from her desk like a gazelle, and barred Nelly's exit from her bedroom.

'OK!' she panted. 'I'll give you five pounds, but you're not allowed to see where I get it from.'

A smile stole across Nelly's face as she closed

her eyes, faced the bedroom door and listened.

Asti crept secretly to a corner of her room, opened the lid of her musical box, took four musical bars of 'The Last Waltz' to remove something from inside, shut the music box lid and returned to Nelly's side.

'OK, you can look now,' she said.

Nelly turned round to find a deliciously crisp five-pound note hovering in front of her eyes. With a businesslike handshake, papers were exchanged and the deal was done.

'I'll hang around in your room for a while,' said Nelly, trotting over to Asti's bed and stretching out on her duvet. She knew if her dad saw her emerge from her sister's bedroom too early, it would look like she hadn't been helping her at all. 'Just in case you get stuck,' she added.

'I'm not paying you any more if I do get stuck,' grumbled Asti, propping the top sheet of Nelly's essay against the wall and then searching inside her pencil case for a biro that hadn't been mullered.

'Fair enough,' said Nelly, holding the five-pound note up to the light.

'It's not a forgery,' said Asti. 'It's got a silver line through it and everything.'

'Just checking,' smiled Nelly. 'Juuusst checking!'

3

Across the landing in Mum and Dad's bedroom, things were going pretty much as Dad had predicted.

'I can't possibly wear any of these clothes this winter, Clifford,' said Mum, pulling a green blouse from the black bag full of clothes and hurling on to the floor.

'Don't they fit?' asked Dad.

'Of course they fit!' said Nelly's mum. 'They fit me perfectly! Are you saying I've put on weight?'

'No, I'm not saying you've put on weight,' sighed her husband.

'Well, what are you saying then?' asked Nelly's mum.

'I'm just saying, why can't you wear them?' sighed Dad, asking the same question he always asked at this time of the year.

'Because they're last season's colours!' said Nelly's mum, yanking a pair of turquoise trousers out of the bag and dropping them to the carpet in disgust. 'Keep up, Clifford. This season's colour is grey. Light greys, dark greys, charcoal greys. Not greens, turquoises and blues. Anyone with an ounce of fashion sense knows that greens, turquoises and blues have totally BEEN and GONE.'

Nelly's dad stared bleakly down at the carpet. The space between the wardrobe and the foot of the bed was littered with last year's colours. Not to mention last year's credit card activity.

'It's going to cost a bomb to replace all these,' he sighed.

Nelly's mum put her hands on her hips and flared her nostrils. 'OK then. You tell me what I'm going to wear this winter,' she said, pointing at a wardrobe empty of everything but hangers.

'I've got some grey work trousers you can borrow,' said Nelly's dad mischievously. 'And a grey jacket and loads of grey socks.'

'I'll ignore that,' said Nelly's mum, winding a turquoise belt into a coil and dropping it back into the bag.

'Or perhaps you'd like me to dress in autumn colours this winter?' she said, pointing at the pile of russets and golds that she had swept from her wardrobe and piled on to the bed.

'I wouldn't mind,' said Nelly's dad, trying in vain to play the flattery card. 'You did look nice in them.'

'Yes, Clifford,' said Nelly's mum. 'In the AUTUMN I looked nice in them because these are AUTUMN colours. September and October are the autumn months, and during the months of September and October, colours like these are in fashion. It is now November, Clifford. November is a winter month, and winter months require winter colours.'

'It's been quite a mild November,' said Nelly's dad, hoping he might be able to use global warming to his advantage. 'The weathermen say we're in for a mild December too.'

But Nelly's mum was having none of it.

'It's not about weather, it's about fashion,' she said. 'It's about colours.'

And that was the end of it.

For the next twenty minutes, Nelly's dad sat slumped on the bed, torturing himself with visions of credit card bills to come.

Meanwhile, Nelly's mum busied herself feverishly.

'Where are the girls?' she asked, applying the final twist to bin bag Number Four.

Nelly's dad lifted his chin from his hands. 'In Asti's room,' he sighed. 'I asked Nelly to help Asti with her homework.'

Nelly's mum's fingers stopped in mid-twist. Nelly helping Asti with her homework? It was unheard of.

'You ARE joking,' she said, completing the twist and adding a twiddle.

Nelly's dad shook his head and smiled ingeniously. 'I threatened to withdraw my taxi services if she didn't.'

'Excellent!' said Nelly's mum, bundling the bin bags towards the door. 'You are clever, Clifford.

Why haven't we tried that one before?'

Nelly's dad congratulated himself briefly and then gazed bleakly at the empty wardrobe. With a tut and a sigh, he lifted himself weakly from the bed and limped towards the door.

'I don't know why you can't buy paper clothes,' he mumbled, picking up the first two bin bags. 'You could buy any colour you wanted, wear it once and then throw it away. We'd save a fortune.'

'You're not talking to yourself again, Clifford, are you?' said Nelly's mum.

'No, love,' fibbed Nelly's dad, limping across the landing and struggling no-handed up the lower steps of the loft ladder.

'I'll bring the other two out for you,' said Nelly's mum helpfully, crossing the landing with a bag in each hand and lifting one up to the height of her husband's ankles. 'I can't believe my wardrobe! It looks so empty!'

'I can,' mumbled Nelly's dad, bundling the first two bags through the hatch and then stooping low to grab hold of the other two.

'I might take Asti shopping with me next

weekend,' chirruped Nelly's mum. 'She loves shopping for clothes.'

'Take Nelly instead,' pleaded her husband, almost losing his footing at the thought of his wife AND Asti running wild with a credit card in the high street.

'Clifford, you know Nelly's not really into fashion,' said Mum. 'She has a fashion sense all of her own.'

Nelly's dad touched down on the landing carpet, and pushed the aluminium loft ladder back up into the roof.

'Why don't you and Asti both develop fashion senses all of your own, like Nelly,' he sighed. 'Then you'd be able to mix and match all the seasons' colours from all the different years. There's a whole roof full of mix-and-match fashion opportunities up there.'

'I'll take Asti,' said Nelly's mum firmly.

With the wardrobe emptied, the clothes bags despatched and the loft hatch closed for another season, Nelly's dad conceded good-humoured defeat and slipped his arm around his wife's waist.

'Shall we see how they're getting on?' he smiled, turning inquisitively in the direction of Asti's bedroom door.

'Nelly helping Asti with her homework? This I've got to see!' smiled his wife.

Nelly's dad's eyebrows jiggled his agreement as he crept towards Asti's door.

'I can't hear them arguing,' whispered Nelly's mum, placing her hand on the door knob and giving it a twist.

'How are you getting on?' she asked, pushing the door open.

The sudden appearance of Mum and Dad in the bedroom seemed to have the effect of administering both daughters with an electric shock.

Nelly sprang like a coiled bedspring from Asti's bed and hurriedly stuffed something into her pocket. Asti's arm shot out like a lightning bolt, grabbed something and shoved it up her jumper.

From the doorway, it was impossible to make out either a five-pound note or an essay, but boy did it look weird.

'Everything OK?' asked Nelly's mum tentatively.

'YES!' blurted the two girls together.

'Is Nelly helping you with your homework?' asked Nelly's dad.

'No,' said Asti.

'YES!' blurted Nelly. 'Yes, I am helping Asti with her homework,' she blustered, 'but not too much and not too little. Aren't I, Asti?' she said, nodding vigorously.

Asti stared at her sister blankly, and then frowned. Surely Nelly WASN'T meant to be helping her?

Unable to work it out, she took her cue from her sister's bobbing head and simply nodded along.

'Good!' said their dad. 'That's what we like to see.'

'You see, the two of you can get on if you try!' beamed Mum, adding her seal of approval.

'Dad'll kill me if he finds out she's paid me!' thought Nelly, desperate for her sister not to spill the beans.

Asti sat at her desk with her mouth open. She was sure Nelly had said that her dad wouldn't want her to help her.

'I'm going clothes shopping next Saturday if you're interested, girls,' said Mum from the doorway.

'No, ta!' said Nelly. She had already overdosed on the colour pink.

'I don't get it,' murmured Asti, switching from a look of blank confusion to a look of deep mistrust.

'What about you, Asti?' said her mum, extending the invitation to Asti's corner of the room. 'Would you like to come shopping with your mum? The winter season is upon us!'

Asti wasn't listening. Asti was fuming.

'Sorry, Asti, I didn't mean to interrupt your homework. You're obviously deep in thought,' said Mum. 'Come on, Clifford, let's leave them to it.'

Nelly's dad nodded and both parents departed from the room with a little wave.

'That's not like Asti,' said Nelly's mum, walking down the stairs. 'She usually leaps at the chance to go clothes shopping. Miracles never cease!'

'We must get the two of them working together more often,' smiled Dad.

The moment her bedroom door had closed, Asti turned to Nelly with a glare.

'I thought you said Dad wouldn't want you to help me with my homework?' she growled, wrenching the essay out from her jumper.

'Did I say that?' asked Nelly, pushing her five-pound note a little deeper into her jeans pocket.

'YES, YOU DID SAY THAT!' snapped Asti, stabbing her pen into the desk and turning ten shades darker than all the pinks in her bedroom combined. 'HE DOESN'T MIND AT ALL! IN FACT DAD **ASKED** YOU TO HELP ME, DIDN'T HE? WHICH MEANS I SHOULDN'T HAVE HAD TO PAY YOU ANYTHING AT ALL!'

'Gotta go!' said Nelly, jumping from the bed and racing to the door. 'My monster sitting phone is ringing!'

4

Nelly flew down the landing, sidestepped into her bedroom, locked the door behind her and dived for her monster sitting phone.

'My hunch was right!' she smiled, lifting the receiver excitedly and slamming it to her ear after the fifth ring.

'Hello! Nelly the Monster Sitter here!' she trilled.

'Hello,' a rather dreary voice replied flatly.

Nelly parked herself excitedly at her desk and waited for the monster to speak again. But to her surprise, it all went very quiet. There were no slurps, no squeaks, no grunts, no 'My name is', 'We live at', or even a 'Would you monster sit for us?'.

All that followed was a yawn.

Nelly waited uncertainly, and then decided to

take command of the conversation. 'Who am I speaking to?' she enquired politely.

'My name is Nowt,' droned the monster.

'Hello, Nowt!' said Nelly brightly.

'Hello, Nelly,' yawned Nowt.

'GIVE ME MY MONEY BACK!' squawked Asti, pounding her fist on Nelly's bedroom door. 'OPEN UP, NELLY! I WANT MY FIVE POUNDS NOW!'

Nelly lowered the receiver and stared irritably at the door handle of her bedroom. If her sister twisted it much harder, it would come off in her hand.

'Go away! I'm on the phone!' she shouted, cupping her hand over the mouthpiece and then removing it to explain.

'Not you, Nowt. I was talking to my sister Asti. She's being a bit of a pain.'

Nowt said nothing.

'Hello?' said Nelly, not at all sure whether the monster was still there.

'Hello,' came another flat reply.

Nelly whipped her eyes in the direction of her rattling door knob, and then back to the telephone receiver. It was no good – she couldn't have conversations in two different directions at once. Especially with a monster she'd never spoken to before.

'Would you excuse me a moment please, Nowt?' she said, deciding she would have to remove Asti from the proceedings. 'I just need to speak to my sister.'

'Of course,' droned the monster with a yawn.

Nelly slammed the telephone on to the desk and ran to the door. With one hand she pulled the fiver from her pocket, with the other she turned the key in the lock and wrenched the door open. Asti was glowering on the landing.

'Will you GO AWAY!' snapped Nelly. 'I'm trying to talk to a new monster on the phone!'

'FIVE POUNDS!' glared Asti, holding out her hand and waiting to be recompensed.

'DINOSAUR ESSAY!' glared Nelly, pressing the fiver back into Asti's palm and then flipping her hand over to receive something in return. 'If you want your five pounds back, then you can give me my essay back too. You can give it back right now, and go back to your bedroom and use your one and only brain cell to do your homework all by yourself without any help from me!'

Asti's fingers snapped around the fiver like a bear trap, but before she could nail Nelly with another glare, Nelly slammed the door in her face and rattled the key in the lock.

'I hope she hasn't hung up!' thought Nelly, racing to her desk again and snatching up her monster sitting phone.

'Hello, I'm back,' she gasped. 'Sorry about

that. Now, where were we?'

There was another yawn.

The yawn grew, extended further, climaxed and then faded away.

'Would you like me to monster sit for you?' asked Nelly, deciding to take the most direct route possible with the conversation.

'Yes,' the monster replied flatly.

'When exactly would you like me to monster sit for you?' asked Nelly, deciding to keep the straight questions coming.

'Whenever,' yawned the monster.

'*Whenever?*' frowned Nelly. She had never had a response like that before! Usually it was a 'Next Saturday' or a 'When are you available?'. Never a 'Whenever'.

She leaned across and slid her monster sitting diary towards her.

'Well, would you like me to monster sit for you sooner or later?' she probed.

'Sooner would be fine,' yawned the voice.

'Or later,' it continued.

Nelly chuckled and then waited patiently for

another yawn to subside. This wasn't the kind of monster sitting enquiry she was used to. But hey, everyone to their own!

She slipped her fingers into her diary like a paper knife and boldly seized the initiative again. 'How about next Wednesday after school then?' she smiled.

'Next Wednesday would be fine,' replied the monster, without the faintest trace of enthusiasm.

'I could do a different evening if you want,' wavered Nelly.

'A different evening would be fine,' yawned the monster. 'You choose.'

Nelly leaned back into her chair. If the monster on the end of the phone needed a baby sitter, it certainly didn't sound like it.

Nelly batted the uncertainty away and stayed positive.

'Wednesday it is then!' she said decisively.

There was a pause, a stifled monster yawn, and then, to Nelly's surprise, a whole sentence!

'Wednesday will be fine,' droned the monster. 'Shall we say seven till ten?'

'I'll need your address,' said Nelly, inching excitedly to the edge of her desk to pluck her gel pen from her pencil case.

'Sour End,' yawned the monster. 'We live at Sour End.'

'Near the river?' asked Nelly, pointing the compass in her brain south-west.

'Yes,' yawned the monster. 'We live at Number Nothing Sour End.'

Nelly's fingers tightened around her gel pen. Number Nothing?

'Errrr . . . what number did you say you live at?' she asked. 'I don't think I heard you properly.'

'Number Nothing,' yawned the monster, 'I live there with my husband Nil and daughter Leavit. Our address is Number Nothing Sour End.'

Another pause followed, only this time it was of Nelly's making.

'You can't miss us,' yawned the monster, leading the conversation for the first time. 'We're in between Number 19 and Number 23. Grey door, grey gates.'

Nelly counted imaginary doors in her head, and then doodled the number zero into her diary.

'What happened to Number 21?' she asked curiously, circling the zero heavily.

'We changed the number 21 to the number Nothing,' explained the monster. 'Nothing is more our style.'

Nelly shook her head. Of all the addresses she had written in her diary, nothing compared to Number Nothing! She circled the strawberry-coloured zero three more times again, and then gathered her senses.

'May I ask what kind of monsters you are, please?' she said, the nib of her gel pen poised.

'We're Polarbores,' yawned the monster.

A blizzard of white blew through Nelly's imagination as the prospect of monster sitting a family of huge white furry beasts with black noses loomed large.

She lowered the nib of her pen to the page of her diary, smiled and then frowned.

'Did you say bears or bores?' she asked.

'Bores,' yawned the reply.

'Ahh,' thought Nelly, underlining the last five letters of the Polarbores' name. The penny was starting to drop. 'You're not bears then?' she asked.

'No, we're bores,' droned the monster.

'Bores as in boring?' asked Nelly, suddenly beginning to make sense of all the sighs and yawns.

'That's right,' came another yawn.

'Bores as in boredom?' quizzed Nelly.

'That's right,' yawned the monster.

'Boring monsters!' gasped Nelly. How on earth was she going to monster sit them?

'Is there anything special you'd like me to bring?' Nelly asked.

The answer was an unexpected 'yes'.

Nelly's pen nib dropped two lines down the page of her diary and hovered excitedly.

'And what would that be?' she asked.

'Nothing,' replied the monster. 'We'd like you to bring nothing. Come to Number Nothing next Wednesday and bring nothing.

'And while my husband and I are away from

the house,' the monster continued, 'we would like you to do nothing.'

The tip of Nelly's gel pen slid across the page like a drunken spider. Bring nothing? Do nothing?

'What, nothing nothing?' Nelly asked.

'Nothing nothing,' came the flat but insistent reply. 'We're Polarbores, you see. There's nothing we Polarbores like doing more than nothing. Do you think you can manage to do nothing with our daughter Leavit, Nelly?'

Nelly took a long and bewildered breath.

'So you don't want me to play with your daughter while you're out?' she asked.

'Oh no,' droned the reply. 'Leavit wouldn't like that.'

'Sing songs?' probed Nelly.

'Definitely not,' droned the monster.

'Or entertain your daughter in any way?' Nelly pressed.

'No,' said the monster. 'Absolutely not.'

'You want me to make my visit as boring as possible?' enquired Nelly, making doubly sure she understood precisely what the Polarbores were asking of her. Or rather weren't asking of her.

'The more boring the better for a Polarbore,' yawned Nowt.

Nelly looked down at her gel pen. The nib had slipped from the page of her diary and was making a big strawberry red ink stain on her quilt cover. She lifted her hand with a start and then caught her breath again as the phone went dead.

Nowt was gone. The phone call was over. There was no goodbye, no 'See you next Wednesday'. No 'Can't wait to see you'. Nothing.

She sat on the edge of her bed for a moment to think things through and then slowly smiled to herself.

'So you like things boring, do you?' she mused to herself. 'Well, Mrs Polarbore, Nelly the Monster Sitter will soon change that!'

She stood up, headed for her bedroom door and smiled again. While she had been talking on the phone Asti had pushed something under her door.

Nelly picked it up from the carpet and tucked it triumphantly into the pocket of her jeans. It wasn't her dinosaur essay. Oh no.

It was the five-pound note!

5

When the school bell heralded the end of the day the following Wednesday, a rather less triumphant Nelly the Monster Sitter stood up from her desk.

Normally when she had monsters to sit, she was ready with her bag packed and out of the door in a flash. But this afternoon, as all her school mates filed left out of the classroom in the direction of the school gates, Nelly filed right, in the direction of the assembly hall.

She was followed by Asti.

'I CANNOT BELIEVE you copied my essay WORD FOR WORD!' fumed Nelly.

'Oh, shut up,' said Asti, traipsing along the corridor towards the detention zone. 'You said I could copy your essay, so I copied it.'

'Not word for word I didn't!' said Nelly,

dropping her voice as the head of year passed them with a frown.

'How was I to know Mrs Boilie would spot the similarities?' protested Asti.

'SIMILARITIES?' gasped Nelly. 'Our essays were identical! Plus our teachers are identical!! That's how!'

Asti tugged the strap of her school bag higher up her shoulder and flounced past a long line of school lockers. 'We're twins, aren't we?' she growled. 'If twins can't do things identically then who can?'

'WE'RE NOT IDENTICAL TWINS, YOU MUPPET!' snapped Nelly.

'Thank God for that!' said Asti. 'I'd hate to be identical to you.'

'I'd hate to be identical to you,' said Nelly.

'I wouldn't want to be in the very slightest way the same as you,' said Asti.

'I wouldn't want to be in the very slightest way the same as you,' said Nelly.

'I wish you'd been a brother,' said Asti.

'I wish you'd been a brother,' said Nelly.

The two sisters entered the assembly hall with identical scowls on their faces and took their seats alongside each other in the middle of the detention zone.

Mr Sturgis, the head teacher, was already seated at the sharp end of a triangle of desks.

'Aaahhhhhh!' he ahhed. 'If it isn't the Amazing Synchronized Morton Sisters.'

Keen to avoid as much eye contact as possible, Nelly and Asti stared down at their desks. Four pristine sheets of A4 lined paper lay before them.

Mr Sturgis continued. 'Mrs Boilie tells me that your dinosaur homework essays, although commendable in one way, were identical in every other way. Is this true?'

'Yes, sir,'/'Yes, sir,' said Asti and Nelly together.

'Is there an illuminating explanation for this that escapes me?' purred Mr Sturgis, torturing his two detention victims with as much wordcraft as he could muster. 'Was Mars in line with Jupiter and Saturn in line with Neptune and all of the planets in line with both of your biros the moonlit Sunday night that you wrote these essays?'

'No, sir,'/'No, sir,' replied Asti and Nelly with identical nods.

'Did aliens land in your back garden over the weekend, remove the brains that you have been bringing to this school for the past two years, and replace them with new grey matter laboratory-grown from the same petri dish?'

'No, sir,'/'No, sir,' mumbled Asti and Nelly.

'Or have you been COPYING?' he growled, leaning forward across the desk and thumping it with his fist.

Nelly and Asti jumped in unison and then raised their eyes sheepishly to meet his.

'What's another word for copying, Astilbe Morton?' he purred.

Asti racked her brains, but the heat of the moment had melted her vocabulary like candlewax.

'What's another word for copying, Petronella?' he asked, turning his spotlight to Asti's left.

'Cheating, sir,' said Nelly.

'Exactly!' said the head teacher, rising from his desk and leaning forward on his knuckles like a hump-backed sloth. 'CHEATING! And do we tolerate cheats in this school?'

Nelly's eyes dropped, widened, and then turned towards her sister.

Mr Sturgis's fly was undone and his boxer shorts were poking through!

Asti had noticed this too.

The faces of the two girls twitched involuntarily

as they stared solemnly up at the bearded face of
their persecutor.

'No, sir,'/'No, sir,' they squeaked.

Nelly's face reddened. Their head teacher was
wearing Christmas underpants! In November!

Mr Sturgis jutted his chin forward like a
church gargoyle and delivered his holly-leaf-and-
reindeer-underpanted sentence.

'You have one hour to write me an essay
entitled *Cheats Never Prosper. Explain.* Starting
from NOW! And NO CONFERRING!'

Nelly and Asti dived into their school bags,
grabbed biros from their pencil cases and buried
their faces in their desks.

'Are you LAUGHING, Morton?'

'No, sir,'/'No, sir,' came the muffled squeaks
of two girls trying their utmost to stop their
shoulders from shaking.

The head teacher frowned, glanced down at
his flies and turned crimson.

'I have to go to the staff room for a moment,'
he blustered. 'I will be back after my meeting. No
conferring EITHER OF YOU!'

As he beat a hasty retreat from the assembly hall, Asti and Nelly collapsed in hysterics.

'CHRISTMAS UNDERPANTS!' they squealed. Our head teacher wears Christmas underpants! In NOVEMBER!'

'Explain that!' snorted Asti, picking up her pen.

When they finally exited the school gates an hour later the sisters were still beside themselves with laughter.

'I wish I'd got a photo on my mobile!' piped Nelly. 'Then we could have sent it to the entire school.'

'We could have posted it on the internet!' laughed Asti, swinging her school bag exuberantly. 'Then the whole world would know that Mr Sturgis wears . . .'

'HOLLY LEAF UNDERPANTS!'/'REINDEER UNDERPANTS!'

'IN NOVEMBER!'/'IN NOVEMBER!'

It was a rare sight indeed. Not Mr Sturgis's novelty boxers, but the two sisters laughing and joking together. A five-pound note and a detention had brought them closer together than they ever would have imagined. Perhaps their mum was right. Maybe they could get on together, just once in a while, if (and it was a big if) they tried.

6

Asti and Nelly's journey home from school was fun all the way, with the conversation switching halfway along Milk Bottle Close from Mr Sturgis's underpants to the likely appearance of a Polarbore.

Asti, like Nelly, had put 'bore' and 'bear' together and had immediately conjured up images of polar bear-like creatures with four heads, black noses and snowy white shaggy coats. By the time they had passed Candy Close, the four white shaggy bodies had acquired four matching bottoms, and by the time they had reached Jelly Street each of the bottoms was wearing Mr Sturgis style underpants.

They were almost as far as Glee Street before the two of them had stopped chuckling enough to even contemplate what big-time boring monsters might look like. By then, they were almost home.

Nelly looked six houses further along Sweet Street. It was already dark, and her mum had once again forgotten to draw the curtains. As the lounge wallpaper came into focus, she glanced at her watch and put on a spurt.

With a kick of the gate and a twist of her door key, she flew into the house like a whirlwind. She had lost an hour and a half of valuable preparation time and needed to change out of her school clothes and into her favourite monster sitting gear. She also had tea to eat and more homework to do!

Asti caught her up at the top of the stairs.

'If you want to really bore them,' she laughed, 'show them Dad's beer mat collection.'

Nelly hopped across her bedroom floor with one leg of her school trousers on and one off, toppled over and fell on to her bed with a giggle.

'Maybe I'll take Mum and Dad's wedding album!' she shouted, yanking at her tie. 'Or their wedding video!'

'Have you seen the suit Dad wore to get married?' hooted Asti from her own bedroom. 'That's not boring, it's HILARIOUS!'

The chuckles and giggles continued through homework, through teatime, and even through the washing up and drying.

By the time the final saucepan had been removed from the draining board, the girls' parents were in deep shock.

'I've never seen them get on so well,' whispered Mum.

'Me neither,' whispered Dad.

'See you sometime after ten!' shouted Nelly, adjusting her scrunchy in the hallway mirror and pressing a Post-it note to her reflection, somewhere in the area of her chin.

'Don't forget my beer mat album!' shouted Nelly's dad, not realizing the joke was on him.

'Don't worry, I'll take it next time!' chuckled Nelly.

'If you don't die of boredom at the Polarbores'!' hooted Asti.

Nelly's mum and dad exchanged confused

glances. Whatever had got into their two daughters that evening was a complete mystery to them. But oh, how they wished they could bottle it!

Even Nelly, as she hurried along the dark streets into Angelica Way, was a little surprised how she and her sister had suddenly warmed to each other that afternoon.

'Actually, Asti's OK,' she mused. 'Well, *sometimes* she can be OK,' she added cautiously.

Her pulse moved up a gear as she approached Menthol Way.

Two years ago there had been a funny smell about Menthol Way, and it hadn't been the smell of menthol.

Asti, on one of her less charitable days, had said it was the smell of their rival school, Floss Street High, located only two streets further along at the far end of the road. But Nelly had pinpointed it correctly as pollution of the River Hayes. The culprit had been the treacle factory located five miles upstream in the neighbouring town of Blighton Lock. Over a period of high summer months, black treacle had oozed into the river course through a broken pipe, coating fish and plant life alike.

The smell of toffee had hung in the air for months, even carrying as far as the town precinct on particularly windy days. Now, whenever Nelly stepped into Menthol Way, she did so with a sniff.

The air this evening was clean and crisp, just as Nelly liked it.

She threw a couple of casual glances to her right as she passed by Wurly and Curly Street, and then picked up the pace as Floss Street High School drew near.

The rivalry between Floss Street High and Nelly's school was a storm in a pencil case. Given that the two schools were only a mile apart, it was hard to be niggly with children who were practically your neighbours.

Most scuffles after school were blown up out of all proportion, and at weekends any nastiness simply melted away. Not that Nelly was into scuffles after school – she had always preferred to keep her rivalry for Asti.

As the long line of street lamps along Menthol Way began to shorten, she switched her thoughts excitedly to the monster sitting adventure that lay ahead. Boring monsters? How boring could they be? Surely nowhere near as boring as school.

The school buildings she was approaching looked particularly uninviting that evening. A shroud of darkness had draped itself over the school fence, and every classroom in the building was black with after-school inactivity.

Nelly glanced through the open school gates, and then stepped off the kerb at the caretaker's cottage.

She was at the top of Sour End.

'Polarbores, here I come!' she smiled, turning to face the houses that lined the cul de sac and its turning circle at the end.

Located in one of the remotest corners of the Montelimar Estate, Sour End was the perfect home for a Polarbore. Aside from the school run, when bumper-to-bumper cars invaded it, Sour End seldom gave the appearance of being busy.

The houses that lined the cul de sac had been

built in the 1980s from bright yellow bricks, and although Number 3 had given all of its garden up to patio, most of the houses in the cul de sac seemed keen to present themselves in much the same way.

Nelly walked towards the far end of the End, scouring the doors for numbers as she went.

'Seven,' she counted. 'Nine,' she counted. 'Eleven,' she murmured.

Each house in Sour End seemed to be a carbon copy of the other.

Except for Number Nothing.

Even from a distance, and even in the dark, it was clear that Number Nothing Sour End was a house with nothing going for it.

Nelly drew up outside the house and blew a puff of exasperated air into the cold night. Unlike all of the other houses in the road, its yellow brick frontage had been rendered with grey cement.

Nelly raised her eyes up to the grey slate roof and then down at the grey tiles of the front step. At first and second glance, all of Number

Nothing's features were absolutely featureless. The garden wall was rendered grey, the wrought iron garden gate had been primed with grey primer, undercoated with grey undercoat and glossed with grey gloss. Even the large circular house number that had been screwed to the front door had been lacquered with grey lacquer and screwed to the grey panel with grey screws. It was, without a shadow of a doubt, the blandest house exterior she had ever seen.

'I hope there's someone in,' smiled Nelly, entering the Polarbores' front garden and scanning the grey-silled windows for signs of life.

As she stepped from the pavement the grey pavement slabs cut left with her, running like stepping stones across the grass all the way up to the grey front door.

Nelly's pulse quickened again. She loved knocking on the door of a new monster's home.

'Where's the doorbell?' she thought.

'Where's the door knocker?' she thought.

There was no doorbell, no door knocker – nothing.

'Knuckles it is then!' she smiled, waiting for the second hand of her watch to signal seven o'clock precisely, and giving the front door a good rap.

There was a pause, followed by another pause, and a longer still pause before finally, eventually and barely noticeably, the door of Number Nothing slowly opened.

'Hello!' said Nelly, extending a friendly hand, dropping her eyes to knee height and then stifling a gasp.

The monster before her was hovering in the air!

7

Nelly stood with her feet glued to the doorstep. She couldn't believe what she was seeing. The monster standing in the hallway before her was actually hovering, at skirting board height, ABOVE the wire bristled doormat!

She lifted her eyes to the Polarbore's waist level and then higher still in search of a pair of wings. But there were no wings!

There was plenty more for Nelly to stare at. In fact, she couldn't decide where not to stare first!

The Polarbore's body was as long and as slender as a broom handle, and had the faded grey-blue sheen of a washed-out dragonfly. From either shoulder two pairs of grey hairpin arms dangled limply, and from its waist, a pair of knobbly spider-thin legs drooped like twiglets.

'Hello, Nelly. I'm Nowt,' yawned the monster, with a blink of its six eyes.

'Hello, Nowt! I'm Nelly,' said Nelly, with a sparkle in her own.

Nelly exchanged a thin, spider-weight handshake and waited for an invitation to enter the house.

The wait became longer than she expected, as another yawn broke across the broad curve of the Polarbore's giant horseshoe-shaped head.

'Do come in,' droned the monster.

'Thank you,' said Nelly, unzipping her coat.

As the Polarbore reversed through the air, Nelly's gaze dropped to the level of the hallway's chromium plated skirting board.

Not only were Nowt's feet hovering above the floor, they were wearing grey patent leather shoes.

'Maybe they're flying shoes,' thought Nelly, wiping her feet on the doormat, although, to be honest, they looked too boring even to walk in.

'Thanks for coming,' yawned the Polarbore, hovering further backwards down the hallway.

'Thanks for inviting me,' beamed Nelly, stepping into the house and holding out her coat.

'Leave it on the floor,' yawned Nowt. 'Nil and Leavit are in the front room waiting to meet you.'

Nelly put her coat down on the grey carpet and then hung back for a moment to watch her host's shoes glide through the air the full length of the hallway.

'How does she do that?' she thought, closing the front door and hurrying down the hallway in the direction of the front room.

'Maybe I'm about to find out!' she thought. 'If it's magic, maybe they'll give me the spell!'

When Nelly caught up with Nowt she found her standing limply in the middle of the front room hovering alongside the two other members of her family.

'This is Nil and this is Leavit,' droned Nowt, lifting both pairs of arms weakly to introduce her husband and daughter.

'They're hovering too!' thought Nelly, gazing open-mouthed around the room. Apart from a grey lampshade hanging from the ceiling in the middle of the room, there wasn't a stick of furniture to be seen. No sofa, no armchair, no television – nothing!

'Hello, Nil! Hello, Leavit!' said Nelly, nodding

left and then right towards the shorter of the two Polarbores. 'My name is Nelly.'

'We know,' yawned Nil. 'My wife Nowt has informed us of that fact.'

Nelly smiled politely and tried to inject a bit of energy into the room.

'And how old are you, Leavit?' she asked brightly.

'Four,' droned the Polarbore.

'And what do you want to be when you're older?' smiled Nelly.

'Five,' yawned Leavit.

'And then six,' droned Nowt.

'And then seven,' droned Nil.

Nelly smiled back at eighteen unblinking eyes.

'Mmm,' she murmured to herself. 'Maybe this is going to be a little harder than I thought.'

'And . . . where are the two of you going to go while I'm monster sitting with Leavit!' she asked.

'Out . . .' replied Nowt flatly.

'. . . side' expanded Nil.

Nelly smiled weakly. 'Outside? Excellent. That's an excellent place to go. I've just come from outside myself and I can tell you it's positively jumpin' outside in Lowbridge tonight!'

Nowt and Nil turned towards each other and shook their giant horseshoe-shaped heads in unison.

'Then we must ask you to return on another day, Nelly,' droned Nowt. 'We Polarbores don't do "jumping". If there are any levels of excitement outside then we would prefer to remain indoors.'

Nelly's smile slipped from her face and dribbled on to her sardine sweatshirt. She had completely underestimated how boring Polarbores preferred to be.

'Sorry,' she said with a wave of her hand. 'I was only joking. There's nothing going on outside at all in Lowbridge this evening, unless you count a half moon and some stars! In fact, it may even have clouded over by now, so you might not even have to bother looking at them!'

The Polarbores' eyes lit up, albeit faintly, and then dimmed.

'Then we shall require your services after all,

Nelly,' Nowt droned. 'Would it be acceptable if we left now and returned at ten o'clock?'

'Ten o'clock would be more than acceptable,' smiled Nelly.

'Good,' yawned Nil. 'Goodbye.'

With the effortless glides of two skaters moving across invisible ice, both Polarbore parents suddenly air walked out of the lounge and vanished into the hallway.

There were no bedtime instructions, no kisses for Leavit, no mention of pyjamas or toothbrushes – nothing. To Nelly's complete surprise, Nil and Nowt just upped and left, leaving her alone in the lounge with a four-year-old Polarbore, no furniture to sit on, no TV to watch and no games cupboard to raid.

At the sound of the front door closing, Nelly ran to the window and prised open the slats of the grey venetian blind.

She could see Nil and Nowt making slow and ponderous progress across the pavement slabs towards the front gate.

'They're not hovering now,' she frowned. 'Why

are they walking on the floor and not in the air?'

She let go of the blind and turned her attention to Leavit.

'How do you do that?' she said, pointing her finger at Leavit's grey patent shoes.

'Do what?' asked Leavit.

'Stand in mid-air!' laughed Nelly.

'Oh,' yawned Leavit, with a shrug of her spindly shoulders. 'It's just something we Polarbores do.'

8

Nelly made her way to the middle of the room and offered Leavit her hand. To her dismay, Leavit declined to take it and kept her arms dangling limply by her sides.

Nelly put her hands on her hips instead.

'Now then, young Leavit,' she smiled, 'what would you like to do?'

'Nothing, thank you,' yawned Leavit.

Nothing? Nelly wasn't having that!

'Come on, Leavit!' she said. 'I'm Nelly the Monster Sitter. Let's have some fun!'

'No, thank you,' said Leavit, with a shake of her head.

Nelly paused. She couldn't see even a hint of a glimmer in any of Leavit's eyes.

'Are there some games somewhere in the house that we can play?' she asked.

'Ooohh noooo,' frowned Leavit. 'Polarbores
don't play games.'

'Would you like to show me your bedroom?'
asked Nelly, hoping that a journey upstairs might
spark some excitement.

'No, thank you,' droned Leavit.

'What kind of bed have you got?' asked Nelly.

'One that I sleep in,' yawned Leavit.

Nelly chewed her lip. This really was becoming
hard work.

'Would you like me to tell you about MY
bedroom?' she asked.

'No, thank you,' said Leavit.

'Would you like me to tell you about my
family?' asked Nelly.

'No, thank you,' said Leavit.

Nelly folded her arms. The little Polarbore had
no desire to do anything except hover boringly in
the middle of an empty room, with her arms
dangling lifelessly by her sides.

She looked at her watch. The hands said
seven o'clock.

'It must be later than that,' frowned Nelly,

raising the dial to her ear.

'It's stopped,' she sighed, giving her wrist a shake and then pulling her mobile phone from her jeans pocket.

Her phone said ten past seven.

'What's your favourite colour, Leavit?' asked Nelly, returning her phone to her pocket. 'Mine's green.'

'Grey,' yawned Leavit.

'Might have guessed,' sighed Nelly.

'What's your favourite food?' she asked.

'Grey,' yawned Leavit.

Nelly's arms dropped limply to her sides. Grey? How can a favourite food be grey?

'No, I don't mean what colour is your favourite food,' explained Nelly, 'I mean what type of food do you like best in the whole wide world?'

'I only know it's grey,' yawned Leavit, 'and I eat it with a straw.'

'Would that be a grey straw by any chance?' sighed Nelly.

'Yes,' nodded Leavit, with six unblinking eyes.

'But you have no idea what your favourite grey food is called?' sighed Nelly.

'I've never asked,' droned Leavit.

Nelly peered around the empty room. It's amazing how much you want to sit down when there's no furniture around to sit on. She needed to sit down. Badly.

'Do you mind if I sit on the floor?' she asked, stepping backwards towards the wall and sliding her shoulder blades down the boring grey wallpaper.

Leavit shrugged indifferently.

'Would you like to come and sit next to me?' said Nelly, patting the floor invitingly.

'No, thank you,' yawned Leavit.

Nelly sat on the boring grey carpet with her shoulders hunched. Even the silver skirting board had more personality than Leavit. She had asked her if she wanted to play, she had asked her if she wanted to sing, she had asked her if she wanted to talk.

'I've seen more life in a wet tea towel hanging on a washing line to dry,' she sighed, slumping further down the wall.

'Are you sure you don't want to do anything?' pleaded Nelly.

'I'm sure,' yawned Leavit.

'OK then,' said Nelly, folding her arms defiantly and stretching out her legs. 'Have it your way. Let's do absolutely nothing.'

'Thank you, Nelly,' droned Leavit, with a lacklustre twitch of her elbows.

Nelly slackened her shoulders and puffed out her cheeks. She couldn't remember a time when she'd actually tried to do nothing.

The little Polarbore before her was a master of the art. Arms limp, legs dangling, head still, eyes fixed directly ahead, she had the dull and lifeless look of a horseshoe on a stick.

Nelly dragged her eyes from Leavit and studied every featureless feature of the room. Apart from the silver skirting, it was grey all the way, from the grey hinges on the door to the grey fibres in the carpet and the grey laces in Leavit's shoes.

With a despairing sigh, Nelly looked down at laces of her red trainers. For the first time in her life, her shoelaces almost appeared interesting.

Even the eyeholes they were threaded through had something going for them. She raised her knees towards her chest and studied the faded fabric of her green jeans. She dropped her chin to examine the transfer printing on her favourite sardine sweatshirt, and then lifted her eyes to explore the room again.

But there was nothing to explore. No furry wallpaper like the Grerks', no icicles like the Thermitts', no canal bed like the Water Greeps'. Nothing.

'How can anyone possibly live without furniture?' she mused.

'How can anyone possibly survive without a television!'

The Polarbores' home was boring beyond belief!

Nelly prised her mobile phone from her pocket and checked the time. Only two more minutes had passed! This was going to be torture!

Leavit seemed happy enough. A short but contented smile had spread across the lowermost curve of her head, and all six of her battleship-grey eyes had dimmed a little more.

'Are you totally totally sure you don't want to do anything?' sighed Nelly, staring across the carpet at Leavit's bobbly hovering legs.

'No, thank you,' droned Leavit, staring blankly ahead at the wall.

'That's cool,' said Nelly with a grimace. 'Doing nothing is cool with me. Being boring is cool with me,' she sighed. 'If you want to do nothing, we'll do nothing.'

And nothing was precisely what they did. For the next excruciating hour and a half Nelly sat motionless on the floor of the Polarbores' front room, with her back to the wall and her knees hugged to her chest.

Leavit, meanwhile, hovered limply, boringly and contentedly before her in the middle of the empty grey room.

By 8.45 Nelly's brain was ready to explode. The digits on the clock dial of her mobile phone had slowed to the pace of an arthritic slug and her bum had turned to stone.

'I'm actually going to die of boredom,' she winced. 'I never thought that was possible, but I

AM actually going to croak it here and now!'

She released her knees and rubbed her temples. Her brain felt like a balloon that had been overpumped with nothingness.

'I need to think of something to do,' she groaned, 'or my brain is going to pop!'

She stared at her knees. She stared at the walls.

She thought of her school. She thought of her home. She thought of dinosaurs. She thought of her sister.

She couldn't. Could she?

Nelly straightened her legs and dropped her fingers towards her jeans pocket.

With a nibble of her lip, she slipped her fingers inside her pocket.

With an arch of her eyebrows, she closed her fingers around her mobile phone.

With a glance across the carpet, she pulled the phone from her pocket.

With a dry and nervous swallow, she raised the phone to eye level.

With a desperate gleam in both eyes, she slid back the phone cover.

. . .

And dialled home.

9

'Asti! It's Nelly on the phone for you!' shouted her mum from the bedroom.

Asti was curled up on an armchair in the lounge. She lifted her head from her teen mag and turned towards the open door.

'I thought Nelly was monster sitting!' she shouted back.

'She is,' shouted her mum, extending the phone cord to arm's length and walking as far as she could in the direction of the top of the stairs.

'She never rings me when she's monster sitting,' shouted Asti with a frown. Come to think of it . . . 'She never rings me at all!'

'Well, she's ringing you now,' shouted her mum, 'so will you please pick up the phone in the hallway. I need to dry my hair!'

Asti placed her magazine on the arm of the

sofa and walked curiously into the hallway.

'Hello?' she said cautiously.

Sure enough, there was Nelly's voice on the end of the phone.

'Asti!' blurted Nelly. 'You've got to come and help me. It's boring beyond belief round here. There's nothing to do and nothing to say and nowhere to go and no one to talk to.'

'What about the thing you're baby sitting?' asked Asti.

'She won't talk to me!' whispered Nelly. 'She won't do anything!'

'Watch the telly then,' said Asti.

'There is no telly!' whispered Nelly.

'Read a book then,' said Asti.

'There are no books to read! There's nothing here at all. There isn't even any furniture to sit on!' Nelly gasped out.

'So what do you want me to do?' asked Asti.

'I want you to come and monster sit with me!' pleaded Nelly.

Asti's fingers sprang open and she almost dropped the phone.

'I know we don't usually get on,' gasped Nelly, 'but we DID get on this afternoon after school, didn't we, which shows we CAN get on if we try, and I wouldn't normally ask anyone to monster sit with me, least of all you, but this is an emergency, in fact this could be life or death, Asti, because these monsters are unbelievably boring, in fact they're so boring I think I might actually be DYING of boredom, I can feel my brain cells popping, Asti, you MUST come round to Sour End now!'

Asti tightened her fingers around the phone again and furrowed her brow.

'How many heads have they got?' she asked.

'One,' said Nelly, deciding it would probably be best if she didn't elaborate more than that.

'How many legs?' asked Asti.

'Two,' said Nelly, 'the same as you and me! They even wear shoes!'

Asti waited for her initial shivers to pass, and slowly turned the situation over in her mind.

'Don't ask about the arms,' thought Nelly. 'Don't ask about the arms.'

'How many arms have they got?' asked Asti.

'Two,' said Nelly, 'on both sides,' she whispered from the corner of her mouth.

'Four arms?' shuddered Asti. 'You want me to go near something with four arms?'

'They don't do anything,' said Nelly, 'they just dangle. In fact Polarbores don't do anything at all! They just hov— I mean, stand in the middle of the room and do nothing,' she added.

'Is that all?' said Asti cautiously.

'That's all,' whispered Nelly, deciding not to mention the fact that when Polarbores stood anywhere, they did so with both feet off the ground.

'OK,' said Asti, secretly flattered that her sister had actually called upon her for help.

'So long as we come to a little arrangement first,' Asti smiled.

It was Nelly's turn to frown suspiciously now.

'What arrangement?' she asked.

'You can pay ME five pounds this time!' grinned Asti, tingling with the thrill of turning the tables on her sister. 'I paid you five pounds for your essay, you can pay me five pounds for coming to monster sit with you!'

Nelly's bottom slid another couple of centimetres across the carpet. Asti had her over a barrel, and to be honest it was no less than she deserved.

'OK,' she sighed, staring across the carpet at the lifeless monster before her. 'I'll give you your five pounds back.

'But get round here fast!'

10

'Why have you brought our rounders bat with you?' sighed Nelly, opening the door of Number Nothing to her sister.

'Just in case,' said Asti, stepping furtively into the hallway and flashing her eyes in all directions. 'It's a bit grey in here, isn't it?' she murmured, eying up the Polarbores' decor.

'It's *a lot* grey,' groaned Nelly.

'Where's the monster kid?' asked Asti, tightening her grip on the rounders bat.

'In the front room,' said Nelly.

'What's it doing?' asked Asti.

'Nothing,' sighed Nelly, prising the coat from her sister's shoulders and the bat from her hand.

Asti followed Nelly down the hallway and stopped abruptly outside the door to the lounge.

'What's wrong?' asked Nelly.

'Five pounds, please,' smiled Asti, holding out her hand palm.

Nelly sighed again and eased her fingers into the back pocket of her jeans.

'Here you go,' she said, pressing the same fiver into her sister's palm. 'Now we're even.'

Asti folded the fiver into a chewing-gum-sized strip and poked it into her cardigan pocket. 'OK,' she shuddered, 'let's do this.'

'Leavit, this is my sister Asti,' said Nelly,

stepping into the front room. 'Asti has come to keep me company while you do nothing. Is that OK?'

Leavit turned her horseshoe head in the direction of the door, and peered with blank disinterest at the newcomer.

'Hello, Asti,' she droned.

Asti's face turned puce.

'Look at its head!' she squeaked. 'It's like a loo seat!'

Nelly elbowed her sister in the ribs and dragged her by the arm of her cardigan over to the far wall.

'It's got six eyes!' squeaked Asti, hugging the wall so tightly she almost slipped behind the wallpaper.

'I know,' whispered Nelly. 'And it's not an it, it's a she.'

'It's a freak!' squeaked Asti, dropping her eyes and then jumping with the sudden realization that the six-eyed, loo-seat-headed abomination before her was hovering in the middle of the carpet!

'It's flying!' squawked Asti. 'Look – its feet

aren't even touching the floor!'

'I know,' whispered Nelly out of the corner of her mouth. 'Now will you stop stating the obvious, and start being a little less rude!'

'You didn't say it had spider's legs!' shuddered Asti.

'You didn't ask,' said Nelly.

'Yes I did,' Asti squeaked.

'No you didn't.' said Nelly, sliding her back down the wall and placing her bum on the carpet. 'You asked how many legs she had, not what sort of legs she had.'

'Look at its arms!' gasped Asti. 'They're all . . .'

'All what?' sighed Nelly.

'Thin . . . and dangly,' shuddered Asti. 'Are you sure it's not going to do something?' she whispered. 'Are you sure I'm not going to need the rounders bat?'

'Let's ask her,' said Nelly bullishly. 'Leavit, Asti would like to know if you're going to do anything.'

Leavit blinked weakly down at the two sisters sitting on the floor before her with their backs parked up against the wall.

'Ooohh noooo,' she droned.

'Told you,' whispered Nelly.

'Well, if she does, I'll hit her for six,' said Asti, waving an imaginary bat in the air.

'Don't be daft,' sighed Nelly. 'She's a four-year-old child.'

'Child?' squeaked Asti. 'How can you call that thing a child?'

'It was funny at school this afternoon, wasn't it?' said Nelly, deliberately changing the subject.

A smile crept slowly across Asti's face.

'Hilarious!' she smiled, one eye on Nelly, the other on the Polarbore. 'I phoned Natalie to tell her that Mr Sturgis wears Christmas underpants! She nearly wet herself!'

'I nearly wet myself too when I saw them,' whispered Nelly. 'Leavit, would you like us to tell you what happened to Asti and me at school today?' asked Nelly.

'Ooohh nooooo,' yawned Leavit.

'I see what you mean,' said Asti, starting to relax a little.

'How is Natalie?' whispered Nelly. 'Are you still

best friends? I haven't seen her in ages.'

Asti tipped her head to one side. 'We weren't for a while but we are now,' she whispered.

'Why? What happened?' asked Nelly.

'She wanted me to try her brace on, but I wouldn't,' said Asti.

'What – her DENTAL brace?' whispered Nelly.

'Yes,' said Asti.

'That's disgusting!' whispered Nelly.

'That's what I said,' whispered Asti.

'Why did she want you to try her dental brace on?'

'To see how much it rubbed. She said it really rubbed her gums at the back, and that I should see how much it rubbed or I'd never be able to truly understand what she was going through.'

Nelly stared across the room at Leavit's expressionless face. Given the choice between an evening with a Polarbore and an evening with Natalie Dupre, she knew which one she would choose.

'Remember when we used to play dentists?' Nelly smiled.

Asti nodded. 'We used to pretend that the cocktail stirrer was a dentist's drill and the coffee beans were black teeth. How old were we then?' whispered Asti.

'About six, I reckon,' smiled Nelly.

'Do you remember having baths together?' whispered Asti. 'We used to give each other beards with the bubble bath suds.'

'And we used to stick Barbie's ankle down the plughole and pretend she was trapped,' whispered Nelly.

'Do you remember the dens we used to build in the garden?' asked Asti.

'When we put the blanket over the washing line to make a tent?' said Nelly.

'That's right,' whispered Asti, 'and Dad used to pretend he was a grizzly bear and come and attack us.'

'And you hit him with Mum's broom,' said Nelly.

'And he had to go to hospital,' said Asti.

'And have stitches,' said Nelly.

'I used to love it when Dad used to turn us upside down,' smiled Asti.

'Me too,' smiled Nelly. 'He used to tell us he'd turned us into Australians.'

'And then we'd have to hop everywhere,' smiled Asti.

The two sisters conjured silently with their memories for a while and then Asti eased her shoulders a little higher up the wall.

'How does it stay off the ground like that?' she whispered.

'I don't know,' whispered Nelly. 'It's just something that Polarbores do apparently. Except when they're outside. When they're outside they walk on the pavement.'

'Monsters are strange, aren't they?' Asti whispered

'People are stranger,' said Nelly.

'No, I mean it's strange how you can sit in the same room with a monster and in a strange way sort of get used it,' said Asti. 'As long as it doesn't do anything,' she added.

Nelly looked at her sister. Was she actually saying what she thought she was saying?

The two sisters looked at the lifeless Polarbore

suspended above the carpet in the middle of the floor.

'Well, she certainly won't do anything while we're here,' sighed Nelly. 'Shame really. All the other monsters I've monster sat have been brilliant fun.'

'What do you reckon she feels like?' whispered Asti, running her eyes down the blue-grey shimmer of Leavit's broom-handle-thin body. 'You know, if you touched her with your fingers.'

'A bit like a giant dragonfly, I reckon,' whispered Nelly.

'Warm or cold?' asked Asti.

'Warm,' whispered Nelly. 'Even Thermitts are warm-blooded.'

'Are those knees all over its legs or bobbles?' whispered Asti.

'I'm not sure,' whispered Nelly.

'Do you dare me to touch it?' whispered Asti.

'No, I don't dare you to touch it,' sighed Nelly. 'And she's not an it, she's a she!'

'I would, you know,' whispered Asti. 'She doesn't scare me.'

'I should hope not,' sighed Nelly. 'She's a toddler!'

'I could touch her just like that if I wanted,' whispered Asti.

'Big deal,' sighed Nelly.

'I reckon I could easily do monster sitting if I wanted,' whispered Asti.

'Could you?' yawned Nelly.

'Yup,' nodded Asti.

Nelly tipped her head to one side. 'I'll tell you what then. Why don't you do a little bit of monster sitting here on your own while I have a look in the back room to see if it's as empty of furniture as it is in here.'

Asti's eyes swivelled right towards her sister and then back to the grey shoes hovering in the centre of the floor.

'OK then,' she whispered, 'I will!'

Nelly sat with her arms around her knees for a moment. She'd never known her sister be so monster-friendly before!

'See you in a tick then,' she said, straightening her legs, un-numbing her bum and then hoisting herself up from the floor.

'I'm just going to have a look in your back room, Leavit,' Nelly explained, before walking towards the other grey door in the room.

'OK,' yawned Leavit indifferently.

Nelly threw a glance back at her sister and then closed her hand around the door knob leading to the back room.

'Won't be long,' she said, pushing the door open and stepping inside.

It was grey all the way in the back room too. In fact the decor in the back room was identical to the front room, right down to the silver skirting board.

'That must be the kitchen,' thought Nelly, turning from the grey slatted blinds that masked the rear garden windows to face a third and equally uninviting grey door.

'I'll just take a quick peek,' she thought, padding across the grey carpet and giving the grey door handle a twist.

She was right. It was the kitchen. And to Nelly's surprise, it did have kitchen appliances and even furniture. Well, sort of.

A rectangular grey slate-surfaced breakfast bar dominated the middle of the room. There were no stools to sit on but there was plenty of room to hover around.

Although all the obvious mod cons such as toasters, coffee percolators and blender were absent, an array of gleaming engineering equipment was very much in evidence. A grey enamelled industrial lathe was bolted to a sparkling granite work surface on the far wall and a brightly polished angle grinder hung from a silver-grey hook beside the kitchen window.

There was no kitchen drainer, no tap and no pedal bin, but on the long wall to Nelly's right, three waist-high breeze-block troughs were laid out in a line. Pointed with grey mortar and of increasing sizes, they put Nelly immediately in mind of the three bears' porridge bowls! Or was that the three bores?

Nelly glanced back at the door to the front room, and then stepped inquisitively over to the long wall.

Poking out from the sludge-grey contents of each trough was a long grey straw.

'This must be what they eat!' she murmured, leaning over the daddy bore's trough to inspect the shimmering sludge inside. At first glance it could have been mistaken for grey porridge or cement, but on closer inspection a coarser, more fibrous texture was revealed.

Nelly dipped her finger into the mixture and rubbed it against her thumb. It wasn't oats, it wasn't bran, it wasn't cement mix either. It wasn't even moist.

'Iron filings!' she gasped. 'Surely the Polarbores don't eat iron filings!'

She scrutinized the rest of the kitchen. There were no cupboards where other food might have been stored, no storage jars, no cereal packets, no shelves or bread bins or fruit bowls.

'They do!' gasped Nelly. 'They do eat iron filings! Just wait till I tell—'

'NELLLLLLLLLLYYYYYYYYYYYYYYYY!!!!!!!' screeeched a familiar voice from the front room.

'HELLLLLPPPPP, Nelly!' screeeched Asti.

'HEEEELLLLPPPP!!! QUICCCKKKK!!!!!'

Nelly's eyes darted from the troughs to the front room. Something was up with Asti. With a pinch and a rub of her finger and thumb, she wheeled round and raced through the kitchen door.

'HHEELLPP! HEELLPP! HHEELLPP! NELLYY!' squawked her sister at the top of her voice. 'COME QUICK!!'

'Oh no,' thought Nelly. 'What's happened?'

11

Nelly ran into the front room and froze.

To her complete horror. she saw Leavit upside down on her head in the middle of the floor with her legs wriggling dementedly in the air.

'Her head's stuck to the carpet!' squawked Asti.

'What have you done?' gasped Nelly, running to the middle of the room and placing her hands gingerly around the Polarbore's upturned body.

'Nothing!' fibbed Asti.

'If it was nothing she wouldn't be standing on her head, would she?' snapped Nelly.

Asti slapped her hands over her eyes and then peeped out between her fingers. 'It was just a bit of fun. Like Dad used to do with us.'

'You didn't tip her upside down?' gasped Nelly.

'Like an Australian,' nodded Asti.

'But Polarbores don't like being tipped upside down!' shouted Nelly. 'Polarbores don't like doing anything, least of all hopping around pretending they're kangaroos!'

'I'm upside down! I'm upside down!' droned Leavit in a low-pitched monotone drone.

'Help me turn her the right way up again!' cried Nelly, trying to manoeuvre herself into a lifting position without getting a kick in the face from a grey patent leather shoe.

'I've tried,' said Asti. 'She won't budge!'

'WELL, TRY AGAIN!' said Nelly, arching her back and preparing to lift.

Asti ducked low, placed the palm of one hand below the curve of Leavit's chin and the fingers of her other hand around the area of Leavit's hips.

'LIFT!' gasped Nelly.

The backs of both sisters arched and then buckled. It was just as Asti said: Leavit was riveted to the floor.

'She weighs a tonne!' gasped Nelly.

'She didn't when I picked her up,' gasped Asti.

'She was really light when I picked her up.'

'I'm upside down! I'm upside down!' droned Leavit, her eyeballs revolving like a wash cycle.

'Try again!' gasped Nelly, hooking both palms beneath the inside curve of the Polarbore's head and arching her back like an Olympic power lifter.

Asti crouched down and repositioned her fingers as best she could around Leavit's chest.

'LIIIIIFFFFFFFFFFFTTTTTTTTT!!!!!!!' grimaced Nelly, digging her heels into the floor and applying as much upward pressure as she could with the palms of her hands.

'LIIIFFFFFFTTT!!' she groaned again from the corner of pursed lips.

'I'M TRYING!' gasped Asti with space hopper cheeks.

Eyes watering, temples bulging, sinews straining, the two sisters pulled and tugged and wrenched and hoicked, but it was hopeless. Leavit's head was welded to the floor.

'You total idiot!' said Nelly, staggering to the edge of the room and sliding down the wall on to the carpet. 'You total numbskulled pea-brained idiot!'

Asti found a different wall to slide down and folded her arms in a sulk. 'How was I to know that was going to happen?' she said. 'I was only trying to have a bit of fun with it.'

'Fun with it?' shouted Nelly, glaring across the room. 'Does she look like she's having fun? And she's not an it, she's a her!'

Asti stared grimly across the grey carpet. Leavit was in a state of mild hysteria, with her arms outstretched and her spider-thin legs thrashing in all directions.

'I'm upside down! I'm upside down!' she droned.

'I wish she'd stop wanging on,' said Asti.

'Wanging on?' said Nelly. 'You'd wang on if you were upside down with your head stuck to the floor!'

'It's not my fault she's a Polarbore,' said Asti. 'If she'd been normal instead of a freak this wouldn't have happened.'

'Yes, and if you'd been normal instead of a

total sieve-head this wouldn't have happened either,' glared Nelly.

The two sisters sat slumped against opposite walls and watched Leavit's overturned-beetle antics from both sides.

'What's happened to her?' gasped Nelly. 'Why can't we lift her off the floor?'

There were no answers, and if an answer was to be found it certainly wasn't going to come from Asti.

Nelly racked her brains. There had to be a simple explanation. She just couldn't figure out what it was.

'I'm upside down! I'm upside down!' droned Leavit, expending more energy than she had in her entire life.

'I know you are. I know you are,' sighed Nelly, prising her mobile from her pocket to check on the time. It was 9.15. Nil and Nowt wouldn't be back for forty-five minutes.

'We've got three quarters of an hour to sort this out!' frowned Nelly.

Asti screwed her face up and stared sullenly at

her knees.

'I'VE got forty-five minutes to sort this out,' murmured Nelly, racking her brains for a game plan.

With a face like a Polarbore, she stared vacantly across the carpet.

'I know what I'll do!' she smiled. 'I'll ring Grit! Grit's the strongest monster I know. If he can't lift her, no one can!'

12

'I can't lift her,' puffed Grit, releasing his leathery Huffaluk paws from the inner curve of Leavit's head and staggering to the edge of the room for a breather.

On receiving Nelly's emergency phone call, he had sprinted all the way from 42 Sweet Street, only to find that he was as powerless to solve the problem as anyone else.

'But you could lift a bus if you wanted to!' said Nelly.

'I know,' puffed Grit, his hairy Huffaluk chest heaving up and down like a foot pump. 'But I can't lift that little Polarbore.'

'I'm upside down! I'm upside down!' droned Leavit, lashing out with her feet like an Italian footballer.

Nelly budged over slightly as Grit slid his ample

bottom down the grey wall to sit beside her.

'What are we going to do?' she sighed.

Grit scratched his hairy head with all three paws. 'I don't know, Nelly. I just don't know,' he growled.

Asti was past caring. After the arrival of a second monster she had gone into an even bigger sulk.

'What time do you make it, Asti?' asked Nelly.

Asti looked sullenly at her watch.

'Five to nine,' she scowled.

Nelly raised her head. 'Five to nine? It must be later than that. I rang Grit at a quarter past nine.'

Asti pulled the sleeve of her cardigan a little further up her arm and checked again.

'My watch has stopped,' she said.

Nelly lifted her shoulders a little higher up the wall. 'What time do you make it, Grit?' she asked.

Grit lifted the huge hairy wrist of his middle paw and shook his head. 'My watch has stopped too.'

Nelly sprang from the floor and clapped her hands. 'ALL OUR WATCHES HAVE STOPPED!

Apart from the digital watch on my phone!'

Asti and Grit looked at each other across the floor and then waited for Nelly to enlighten them.

'THAT'S IT!' beamed Nelly. 'That's why Leavit is stuck to the floor. Don't you see?'

Asti and Grit frowned. They didn't see at all.

'Leavit doesn't have a horseshoe-shaped head, or a loo-seat-shaped head!' said Nelly. 'She has a MAGNET-shaped head! The polarbores are MAGNETIC! That's why they eat iron filings AND THAT'S WHY THEY HOVER OFF THE FLOOR. IT'S REVERSE POLARITY. WE'VE DONE IT IN SCIENCE, ASTI!'

'Have we?' shrugged Asti, looking disdainfully across the carpet at the upside-down iron-filing-eating freak before her. 'This is totally the last time I go monster sitting EVER,' she murmured.

'If the Polarbores are magnetic,' Nelly explained, 'then their top end will be a different polarity to their bottom end. Like north and south. That's what the polar part of their name refers to! Sooooo . . .' she went on, falling silent for a moment to think things through.

'So . . .' she continued, 'when the Polarbores are upright, their feet and the floor beneath their feet must be poles apart. Say north and south. It's the reverse polarity that keeps them hovering off the floor!'

It was all beginning to make some sense, but there was a lot more thinking to do.

'But . . .' she murmured, 'when you turned Leavit upside down, Asti, the polarity in her head must have been the same as the polarity in the floor. Like north north! north north attracts, you see! That's why she's stuck to the floor! It's magnetic attraction!'

Grit stared blankly at Asti. He wasn't much good at science either.

'Get up! Get up!' said Nelly excitedly. 'Help me work this out.'

Grit and Asti heaved themselves up from the floor and waited for their orders.

'Now then,' said Nelly, 'if the Polarbores are magnetic, then the floor must be magnetized too. That means it must be metal. Iron probably. Lift the carpet, Grit, to see if I'm right!'

Nelly watched excitedly as Grit dropped to his knees in the corner of the room and prised his fingers beneath the carpet.

'It's wooden,' he growled. 'There are wooden floorboards under the carpet.'

Nelly's face fell. That wasn't what she expected at all. 'Let me see,' she said, running to the corner of the room to join him.

Grit lifted the carpet a little higher and leaned back to give Nelly room for an inspection. Nelly's eyes bored into the floorboards, and then darted to the underside of the rug.

'Wait a moment,' she murmured. 'Let me read that label.'

Grit's solitary eyeball swung like a tomato on a stalk beneath the upturned carpet. Sure enough, a large label was stitched to the underside.

It read: QUALITY AXMONSTER. Made from 100% Magnithread.

Nelly clapped her head again. 'The floor isn't magnetic, BUT THE CARPET IS! See, it says here on the label that it's made from magnithread! Magnithread must be like magnetic wool!'

Asti stared into space. This was worse than school.

Nelly ran to the middle of the carpet and dropped down on to her knees. 'Don't worry, Leavit,' she smiled. 'We'll have you back on your feet in a moment.'

Leavit's eyes spun in all directions at once. 'I'm upside down! I'm upside down!' she warbled.

Nelly wrenched her mobile from her pocket and checked the time again. It was ten to ten. Nowt and Nil were only ten minutes away now!

'We need to change the polarity in the carpet,' said Nelly. 'From north to south or south to north.'

'How are we going to do that?' asked Grit.

'I don't know,' frowned Nelly, sliding dispiritedly down the wall.

'Brilliant!' hissed Asti. 'All that north south polar gobbledygook stuff for nothing!'

Nelly ignored her and ran her eyes around the four corners of the carpet.

She looked round again, this time a little higher, at the level of the silver skirting board.

She stared at the skirting board for a moment and then stroked her cheek with her fingers.

'Why isn't the skirting board grey like everything else in the house?' she mused.

She examined the skirting board again.

'That's not a switch, is it?' she said, squinting across the floor just to the right of where Asti was sitting.

Asti looked sullenly down to her side and half nodded, half shrugged. Barely noticeable against the chromium-plated silver surface of the skirting board was a small rectangular chromium-plated switch. It was the size and shape of an electric power point, only there was no evidence of a plug or a socket.

'No socket? Just a switch?' frowned Nelly. 'So what does it switch on?

'Does it say anything on it?' she said, getting up from the carpet for a closer inspection.

'It says Ner,' mumbled Asti.

Nelly ran to the opposite side of the room and knelt down by the silver switch.

'It doesn't say N, you doughnut, it says

North!' She clapped. 'And if I push the switch the opposite way,' she mumbled, flicking the switch and pressing her cheek flat against the carpet to gain a view of the underside, 'it says S for South!'

'Look, Nelly!' yelled Grit. 'Look what's happened to Leavit!'

Nelly lifted her cheek from the floor and threw a triumphant glance across the carpet.

Leavit was still upside down, but her head had separated from the carpet and was now hovering at skirting board level.

'The switch on the skirting board switches on the magnetic field in the carpet!' laughed Nelly. 'The polarity in the rooms works at skirting board level!'

'You're right, Nelly!' growled Grit, not understanding a word she'd said but pointing with all three arms excitedly to the middle of the floor. 'The moment you pressed that switch, her head lifted from the floor!'

'Yee-hah!' shouted Nelly. 'Now she's up . . . now she's down!' she laughed, unable to resist another flick of the switch.

'Ahem!' growled Grit sternly. 'We've no time for fun and games, Nelly – Nil and Nowt will be arriving any moment now!'

'You're right!' said Nelly with an apologetic cough. 'Sorry, Leavit,' she added, flicking the switch back to the S position and releasing the Polarbore's head from the floor.

'We still need to turn her the right way up,' she went on.

'I'm not going anywhere near that freak again,' growled Asti.

'Leave it to me, Nelly,' said Grit, lumbering over to the centre of the room and placing a delicate paw – top, middle and bottom – around Leavit's broom-handle body.

'Here she goes!' growled the Huffaluk.

Nelly watched with relief as the wriggling soles of Leavit's shoes arced through the air and welded themselves fast to the floor.

'I'm the right way up! I'm the right way up!' droned Leavit.

'But she's still stuck to the floor!' groaned Grit.

Nelly smiled. 'So now I flick the switch back to N!'

Nelly was right. The instant she returned a northern polarity to the carpet, Leavit's grey patent leather shoes lifted off the floor.

As her feet rose, the eyebrows of all three monster sitters rose with her.

'She's back to normal!' cheered Nelly. 'Now scram the both of you, before Nil and Nowt get back!'

'Good riddance!' scowled Asti, scrambling up from the carpet and giving a wide berth to the upright Polarbore as she hurried from the room.

'To all of you!' she scowled, glaring at Grit and Nelly.

'Do you think she'd like me to walk her home?' smiled Grit as Asti slammed the front door of the Polarbores' house behind her.

'Something tells me not!' laughed Nelly. 'Now run home yourself or I'll get found out!'

'Sorry I couldn't have been more help,' growled Grit, turning his red furry shoulders sideways to squeeze through the grey frame of the hallway door.

'If you hadn't prised the corner of that carpet up, I'd never have seen that Magnithread label!' shouted Nelly after him.

With a slam of the door, Grit was gone.

With a puff of her cheeks, Nelly slid to the floor.

13

The following three and a half minutes passed by blissfully uneventfully. Nelly sat, heart pounding, with her back to the wall staring vacantly into space. Leavit returned to her usual boring self, hovering in the middle of the carpet, arms limp, feet dangling and eyes unblinking.

When Nil and Nowt returned to Number Nothing Sour End at ten on the dot, there was no evidence at all of the drama that had unfolded earlier.

'Have you had a lovely boring time?' asked Nil, pointing three of his unblinking eyes at his daughter and the remaining three at Nelly.

'Asti turned me upside down,' droned Leavit before Nelly had had even half a chance to fib.

Nelly scrambled to her feet.

'YOU'VE GOT SOMETHING ON YOUR

BACK!' she blurted out, deflecting the Polarbore parents' attention away from their daughter.

'AND YOUR FRONT!'

Nil and Nowt hovered limply in the room and looked awkwardly over their shoulders.

'It's a biro,' said Nelly, prising a ballpoint pen from the back of Nowt's magnetic head. 'And a keyring,' she said, plucking another metal object from the top of Nil's head.

During the course of the Polarbores' walk outside their house, an accumulation of metal objects had stuck to their magnetic bodies. There were paperclips, two front door keys, nine ballpoint pens, a compass and three prefect badges.

'Where did you go for your walk?' asked Nelly, removing each object in turn, like prickly burrs. 'It wasn't the school at the end of the road by any chance, was it?'

Nowt nodded her head. 'We didn't want to go far, Nelly, and the bright lights of the town looked far too exciting, so we decided to remain in the close vicinity.'

'So you went to the school playing fields?' asked Nelly.

'Oh, don't say that,' shuddered Nil. 'We had no idea they were that exciting.'

'We wouldn't have gone anywhere near them if we'd realized they were fields of play.'

'Polarbores don't play, do they?' said Nelly, shaking her head sympathetically.

'Ooohh noo,' droned Nowt. 'Polarbores don't do anything.'

'Well, it's time for me to do something,' said Nelly. 'It's time for me to go home.'

Nil and Nowt watched blankly as Nelly walked to the middle of the room and planted a kiss on the side of Leavit's magnet-shaped head.

'Sorry about the fun and games,' she whispered.

'Goodbye, Nelly,' droned Leavit.

With a sigh and a wave, Nelly saw herself out.

And that was the last Nelly ever saw of the Polarbores. She often wondered whether Leavit had ever mustered the energy or the vocabulary to explain to her parents exactly what had happened while they had been away. Somehow she doubted it.

She doubted, too, whether the Polarbores would ever leave their house again. Now that they knew that bright lights, playing fields and other potential possibilities for excitement lay outside, they would never risk venturing away from their home again.

As monster sitting adventures went, Nelly's introduction to the Polarbores hadn't really gone to plan at all. On the negative side, the introduction of Asti had been a total disaster. Nelly would never invite her sister to join her in a monster's house again, even if her life depended on it.

On a positive note – and it was a small positive – Nelly at least had nine more biros, three prefect badges and fifty-seven paperclips to add to her pencil case!

By the time she walked through the refreshingly red door of her own home that evening her relationship with Asti had returned to its usual poisonous self.

The two of them went clothes shopping

together with their mum the following Saturday but didn't speak a word to each other all day. To their mum's surprise and their dad's relief, neither could find one item of clothing they wanted to buy either.

For some reason, known only to the two girls, the colour grey had no attraction at all.

1

'There it is again!' screamed Nelly's mum, jumping like a circus performer on to the kitchen worktop and hiding her feet behind the sugar bowl.

'DAAAAAD!' shouted Nelly from the breakfast bar. 'Mum's seen that mouse again!'

Nelly's dad stared into his shaving mirror and flicked a dollop of whiskers and foam into the bathroom sink. 'Not THAT mouse again!'

THAT mouse was becoming the bane of his life.

'Can I just finish my shave?' he shouted. 'I'm covered in soap.'

'GET DOWN HERE RIGHT NOW, CLIFFORD!' growled Nelly's mum. 'I am not sharing my house with a mouse!'

Nelly dug her spoon back into her cornflakes and waited for her dad to appear. 'It's only a mouse, Mum,' she reasoned. 'I'd much rather share my house with a mouse than an Asti.'

'Where is Asti?' asked Nelly's mum. 'She'll be late for school if she doesn't come down for her breakfast soon.'

Nelly juggled briefly with thoughts of Asti and the mouse and decided to give the mouse her undivided attention. 'Did you know mice have collapsible skeletons?' she said. 'They can squash their skeletons right down like a flat-pack cardboard box,' she explained. 'That way, they can squeeze under the tiniest of gaps.'

Nelly's mouse expertise wasn't helping.

'Clifford! Get yourself down those stairs NOW!'

'They can squeeze under doors,' continued Nelly, 'or through tiny cracks in a wall. Or that space there,' she said, pointing to the gap under the microwave. 'They could easily get under there. Or the fridge or the washing machine. Mice are totally amazing.'

'Yes, and they're totally incontinent too,' said Nelly's mum.

'What does incontinent mean?' asked Nelly.

'It means they wee everywhere,' said her mum. 'All of the time, everywhere they go, they leave a trail of wee and germs behind them.'

Nelly was impressed. Not with a mouse's incontinence but with her mum's unexpected knowledge of the subject.

Nelly's dad limped into the kitchen with a bath towel draped around his neck and a razor in one hand.

'What are you going to do? Shave it to death?' said Nelly's mum.

'You mustn't kill it!' gasped Nelly. 'It's only a cute furry mouse!'

Nelly's dad looked warily at his wife and daughter. He was about to be sandwiched, and in all probability, crushed in a mouse debate. Should the mouse live or should the mouse die? Right now all he cared about was finishing his shave and leaving for work.

'I was thinking we could buy some of those mouse-friendly traps,' he said, trying to please them both.

Nelly's mum frowned. She didn't much care

for the sound of 'mouse-friendly' but she was wholeheartedly in favour of the word 'traps'.

'I've heard they're quite effective,' Nelly's dad continued. 'I'm not exactly sure how they work, but I believe they catch the mouse alive and unharmed.'

'And THEN what?' said Nelly's mum, folding her arms.

'What do you mean?' asked Nelly's dad.

'I mean, and THEN what do we do with it after we've caught it?' said Nelly's mum.

Nelly's dad looked to Nelly for help with an answer.

'Then I buy a cage for it and keep it as a pet in my bedroom!' said Nelly. 'We could catch two and then they could have babies! I could become a pet mouse breeder! I could start a pet shop!!'

This wasn't the kind of help Nelly's dad needed at all.

'I'll go and hurry Asti up,' he whispered, beating a quick and limping retreat up the stairs.

2

'Kill it!' said Asti. 'Anything that enters our house without Mum's permission deserves to die.'

Asti had at last finished with the hair straighteners and had made her way downstairs for breakfast. Having been warned by her dad about the trouble brewing downstairs, she had decided to seize the chance to forge an international alliance with her mum.

'It's only a mouse!' said Nelly, dropping her empty cereal bowl into the sink.

'Yes, and you're only a furry freak lover,' said Asti. 'If Mum doesn't want a mouse in the house, you shouldn't either. Mum's word should be final.'

Nelly's mum blew the steam from her cup of coffee and smiled appreciatively at her supportive and hair-straightened daughter. Asti smiled back sweetly.

'You are such a loser,' Nelly rasped. 'I'd rather have a rabbit for a sister than an evil airhead like you.'

'Mum, did you hear what Nelly just called me?' whimpered Asti.

Nelly's mum dunked a Bourbon biscuit into her coffee and stared at the gap beneath the microwave.

'I don't care how you get rid of it, Clifford,' she said. 'Just get rid of it.'

Asti nuzzled up closer to her mum. 'Sorry about the other two,' she whispered. 'I can't believe how unsupportive they're being.'

Nelly's mum despatched the Bourbon biscuit in two chomps and then switched her gaze to the gap under the cooker.

Asti put her hand into the biscuit tin and passed her mum a custard cream.

'I just want you to know that as long as there's a mouse in this house, I'll be there for you,' she simpered.

'Thanks, love,' sighed her mum.

'If you like,' cooed Asti, 'I could stay off school

today and look after you, just in case the mouse comes back.'

Asti's mum turned with a no-nonsense stare.

'I'll go and get my school bag,' said Asti hastily, sensing that she had milked the mouse scenario as much as she possibly could.

'Good idea,' muttered her mum.

'I'll buy some mousetraps in my lunch break,' said Nelly's dad, slipping on his jacket, and limping towards the front door.

'Good idea,' growled his wife.

3

When Nelly's dad returned home from work that evening, Nelly was the first to greet him.

'What traps did you get?' she asked. 'You aren't going to splat it, are you?'

Nelly's dad handed her a brown paper bag and yanked his tie loose from his collar. 'They're mouse-friendly ones,' he whispered, 'but don't tell your mum.'

Nelly smiled and then peered inquisitively inside the bag. 'How do they work?' she said. 'Do we have to use cheese?'

'Cheese or chocolate,' whispered her dad. 'I'll show you how they work in a minute.'

'I saw it again, Clifford!' said Nelly's mum, emerging from the lounge. 'Well, half saw it out of the corner of my eye when I was watching the lunchtime news! I saw its horrible scurrying shape shooting along the skirting board beside the fireplace.'

'Is it a field mouse or a house mouse?' asked Nelly, following her mum back into the lounge.

'I don't know!' said Nelly's mum. 'It didn't introduce itself! I barely had time to see it at all before it scooted along there, scurried across there and shot out over here.'

Nelly's dad took the brown paper bag back from her and opened it.

'Voila! Not one, but four Morton Mouse Muggers!'

Nelly's mum peered into the bag and frowned at four grey plastic tubes.

'They don't look very mouse-trappy to me,' she murmured.

'That's the genius of them!' said Nelly's dad. 'It is precisely because they look so ineffective that they ARE so effective. Mice don't hesitate to fall for these!'

'Tell Mum how they work,' said Nelly, keen to find out herself.

'Well,' said Nelly's dad, lifting a trap expertly

from the bag and handing the rest to Nelly. 'You see, this little hinged door at the front of the tube can slide up or down. When it's up like this, the mouse can crawl into the tube.'

Nelly and her mum watched as Dad used his fingernail to flick the grey plastic door open.

'But when the mouse crawls inside the tube the whole thing tips forward, causing the door behind it to close. Because there's only one way in and no way out, once the door is closed the mouse is trapped inside!'

Nelly smiled at the brilliance of the Morton Mouse Mugger, but then looked worriedly at her mum. Her mum seemed far from convinced.

'Why would a mouse want to crawl inside a grey plastic tube?' she asked.

Nelly's dad slapped his forehead. 'Doh! I forgot to say! You have to put bait inside at the back of the tube. "Cheese or chocolate," the man in the hardware store said.'

'Cheese,' said Nelly's mum firmly. 'You keep your hands off my mint Aero!'

'Can I put the cheese in?' said Nelly, skipping

into the kitchen. 'And can I set the traps?'

Nelly's mum raised her eyes from the tube and looked suspiciously at her husband.

'Nelly's changed her tune, hasn't she? This morning she was forming the Save the Mouse Society, and now this evening she can't wait to bait the traps. Am I to assume then that these are the mouse-friendly variety of trap?'

Nelly's dad avoided eye contact and peered down at the tube.

'Not at all,' he fibbed. 'They're lethal to mice, these are. If a mouse steps into this tube, then it's curtains for him,' he said, drawing his fingers across his throat like a knife blade.

Nelly's mum smiled and drew her knight in shining armour towards her.

'I've got some cheese!' said Nelly, interrupting a potentially embarrassing mother/father moment.

'That's my favourite cheese!' whined Asti, chasing Nelly out of the kitchen. 'Why does Nelly have to use MY favourite cheese!'

Nelly tightened her grip on the cheese packet

and winked at her dad. 'Because, Asti, it says in the mousetrap instructions *For maximum mouse capture use Freshco's extra mild Cheddar ready-cut sandwich slices.* That's why.'

Asti screwed up her face.

'But they're the last two slices!' she said, stamping her foot. 'What am I going to have on my crispbreads at school tomorrow?'

'If you ask Snowball nicely, he might let you try some of his Bunnymix,' smirked Nelly with a twitch of her nose. 'Actually, why not put some hay in your sandwich box? It's got to be tastier than crispbread.'

Nelly's mum and dad looked at each other and sighed. If there was anything to argue about in this house then you could be sure Nelly and Asti would be arguing about it.

'Just set the traps!' growled Nelly's mum. 'And if any of you so much as breathe on my mint Aero, you will die too!'

4

As Nelly lay in the darkness of her bedroom that night, a tingle of excitement fizzed through her. Just think, by tomorrow morning she could be the owner of a new pet!

Nelly rolled over and peered through the shadowy gloom in the direction of her bedroom door. She had persuaded her dad to let her put a mousetrap in her bedroom. It was tight up against the skirting board, just to the right of her school bag.

She rolled over on to her back and placed her arms on top of her quilt.

'If I catch a mouse, I'll call it Cheesy,' she thought to herself. 'No – Whiskers. No – Cheddar.'

With a plump of her pillow and a big yawn, she closed her eyes.

'What's a good name for a pet mouse?' she mumbled dreamily. 'What's a reaalllllly good name for a pet mouse?'

'Mickey?' she yawned

'Squeaky?'

'Squeak?'

'Tails?'

'Nipper?'

'Chink?'

Nelly opened her eyes.

Chink

Chink

Chink chink chink chink chink

That wasn't a name, that was a noise.

A rather curious noise?

Nelly rolled over and squinted curiously in the direction of her bedroom door.

There it was again.

Chink chink chink, like the sound of a tiny letter box opening and shutting.

Nelly held her breath and listened harder still. In a strange way, the darkness of the room made the sound easier to locate. It was definitely coming from the other side of her room; not high up near the ceiling, but low down near the floor.

With the stealth of a panther in pyjamas, Nelly slid from under the duvet and lowered her feet to the carpet.

She sat for a moment on the edge of her bed and listened hard.

The noise stopped.

Then it restarted. Only this time a little bit louder and faster too.

Nelly put her hand over her mouth to stop herself from whooping with excitement.

The *chink chink chink* was coming from direction of the Morton Mouse Mugger!

'It's worked!' she gasped. 'My trap has caught THAT mouse!'

She stood up in a bit of a panic, sat down on her bed, stood up, and sat down again. What was she to do? Should she call for her dad? No, she couldn't do that. Her dad was downstairs with her mum. What if her mum came upstairs with him? Or instead of him? If her mum discovered she'd caught THAT mouse, THAT mouse would be mincemeat.

She felt under her bed with her toes and retrieved her slippers.

THAT mouse was a job for Nelly and Nelly alone!

Nelly tiptoed excitedly through the darkness of her bedroom, and placed the flat of her hand against the door frame. The *chink chink chinking* had grown louder now, and if she wasn't mistaken there was a *scrabble scrabble scrabbling* sound too!

With a slide and a fumble she located the light switch.

'Here goes,' she whispered, flicking the light switch on.

The darkness vanished from the bedroom in a blink.

With a double blink of her own, Nelly looked down at the floor and then dropped to her knees to investigate the small grey tube.

She was right! She must have caught a mouse! The small hinged door at the entrance of the tube had dropped shut, and the scrabble of tiny claws could be heard faintly inside.

Slowly, carefully, cautiously, Nelly placed the tip of her index finger beneath the lip of the closed hinged door. Hardly daring to breathe, she raised the door the height of a crispbread and took a heart-pounding peek inside.

'Now then, little fella,' she whispered to the tube, 'why don't we say hello?'

'Hello,' replied a voice from inside the tube. 'Are you Nelly the Monster Sitter?'

5

Nelly dropped the mousetrap with a squeak.

'Oi! Be careful!' said a small furry monster as it rolled out on to the carpet. 'I might be tough, but I don't bounce!'

Nelly's eyes bulged. It was the tiniest monster she had ever seen!

'Well?' said a tiny pair of pink lips topped with a yellow moustache.

'Well what?' gasped Nelly.

'I asked you a plain and simple question before you dropped me like a hot chestnut on to the floor,' continued the monster. 'Am I or am I not talking to Nelly the Monster Sitter?'

Nelly knelt down on her bedroom carpet and stared back goggle-eyed.

'Er, yes,' she murmured. 'Yes, you are. I mean, yes, I am. I mean, yes, yes, I am Nelly the

Monster Sitter!'

'Pleased to meet you,' said the monster, extending a small but muscular paw. 'Your reputation has spread far and wide amongst the monster fraternity, Miss Monster Sitter. I was rather wondering whether my wife and I could engage your services for an afternoon?'

Nelly took the tiny paw between her thumb and index finger and shook it delicately. It was a bit like shaking hands with a mole.

'Why didn't you ring?' asked Nelly rather dumbly. 'All my other monster friends ring me on my monster sitting phone.

The monster's berry red eyes began to water

with laughter, and a shrill peeping chuckle whistled from its furry cheeks.

'I might be strong, but I'm not sure I could lift one of those!' he chortled, pointing high up above his head to Nelly's monster sitting phone. 'And anyway, we're not on the phone! That's why I've had to come all the way over here to ask you my very self, in person!'

Nelly looked at her monster sitting phone and realized her mistake. The receiver alone was longer than the monster – more than twice its length!

With an apologetic nod, she leaned lower still and brought her own eyes as near as she could to carpet level.

'Sorry about the noise,' said the monster, casually opening and closing the door of the mousetrap with a *chink chink chink.* 'I thought it would be a good way to get your attention.'

Nelly watched the stubby three-clawed paws toy with the plastic door and then smiled a broad and excited smile.

'Well, it certainly did that!' she whispered. 'I

thought you were a mouse! My whole family thinks you're a mouse!'

'A mouse!' laughed the monster, raising its paws and turning full circle on the spot. 'Do I look like a mouse?'

Nelly shook her head vigorously. Although the tiny monster before her had a body the size of a mouse, it had the hourglass shape of a duckling, the curly tail of a pig, and right down the middle of its back it had the stripe of a blue and white skunk.

'What kind of monster are you?' she whispered, keen not to cause any more offence.

'I'm a Digdigg,' said the monster, 'and my name is Claudius.'

'Pleased to meet you, Claudius,' Nelly whispered. 'How far have you come?'

'A few acres – half a dozen streets or so. We've got a small place on the Crabtree Farm Estate,' said the monster, placing his arm casually across the top of the tube. 'Underground air shelter, it is. World War Two construction. Very cosy, very secure; been in the family fifty years or more. Bit of a find really, if you can find it.'

Nelly traced the Digdigg's journey in her mind.

'To get here from Crabtree Farm, you must have crossed the river, the marshes, the railway line, and even the high street!' she gasped.

'Three out of four!' smiled Claudius. 'We live on the marsh side of the river.'

'How long did it take you to get here?' Nelly whispered.

'Oh, not long,' said Claudius modestly. 'We Digdiggs can put on a bit of a spurt when we need to.'

'But there are hawks on the marshes,' said Nelly, 'and dogs tied to lamp posts in the precinct, and cats in hundreds of the gardens all over the estate! It must have been a really dangerous journey. In fact, be extra careful, Claudius – there's a really nasty cat living right next door. He kills birds all the time,' she exclaimed.

'I know. He's called Barney,' said Claudius. 'I think he's changed his ways.'

'What? You've met him?'

'We had a bit of a chat, yes. Bit of a coward actually.'

'So you weren't frightened at all, at any time, at any point in your journey?' asked Nelly.

'Don't know the meaning of the word,' smiled Claudius.

Nelly rested her cheek on the carpet and smiled a sideways smile at her tiny new monster acquaintance. 'Well, I must say, I'm very pleased to meet you, Claudius. And yes, I would be absolutely delighted to come and monster sit for you and your family. Would you like to meet the rest of my family too?'

Claudius's pencil-line moustache stiffened like a streak of mustard. 'That's very kind of you, Nelly, and I'm sure your family are a delight . . .'

'Asti not included,' thought Nelly.

'It's just that we Digdiggs are a bit of a secretive lot.'

'I understand,' said Nelly, dropping her voice to sub-whisper level.

'Can you keep a secret, Nelly?' said Claudius. 'I'm hoping you can.'

Nelly's cheek brushed softly against the carpet as she nodded.

'Good,' said Claudius, clambering up the collar of her pyjamas and placing his yellow furry snout right inside her ear.

'Our home on the marsh is a bit of a secret too, Nelly,' he whispered. 'Even the farmer doesn't know that we live there. It's important that it stays that way, Nelly, because . . . well . . .'

Nelly waited for Claudius to remove his whiskers from her ear before nodding sideways again.

'I understand,' she whispered. 'If someone finds you, you might lose your home.'

'We might lose our lives!' said Claudius, frowning.

'But if your home is so hard to find, how am I going to find you?' asked Nelly.

'I'll meet you by the Crabtree River Bridge,' said Claudius, 'and lead the way from there.'

Nelly lay on her bedroom carpet and mentally punched the air. How cool was this? Secret mini monsters! She could hardly wait!

'When would you like me to meet y—?'

Nelly's eyes looked at the carpet, but the Digdigg was already halfway under the door.

'I need to get home,' said Claudius, his red berry eyes peering back at her from the tiniest of gaps. 'Could you meet me at the Crabtree Bridge at one o'clock next Sunday?'

'No problem,' whispered Nelly. 'Do I need to bring anything special?'

'Rubber boots and a big stick,' said Claudius, reversing out of sight. 'The marshes can be mighty boggy.'

'I remember,' Nelly nodded. 'We used to go for family walks over by the river when I was little. Wellies are no problem and I'm sure I can find a stick somewhere.'

'Next Sunday it is then,' said Claudius. Only the tip of his nose was visible now.

'Claudius!' whispered Nelly, pressing her cheek flat against the floor. 'I forgot to ask you something.'

Two tiny scarlet eyes reappeared from under the door, just centimetres from her own.

'Ask away,' said Claudius.

'How many children have you got?' whispered Nelly.

'One hundred and twenty,' said Claudius.

Nelly's eyelids shut tight. 'ONE HUNDRED AND TWENTY?'

'And one on the way,' added Claudius before vanishing from view.

6

The following morning Nelly announced proudly to her family that there was no more mouse in the house, that THAT mouse had been caught, and THAT mouse had been despatched by none other than Nelly the Mouse Catcher in person.

As you might expect, Nelly's inability to produce an exterminated mouse as a trophy had raised a considerable number of eyebrows and doubts.

'What did you say you did with the mouse's body?' her mum asked.

'I fed it to Barney next door,' Nelly fibbed, spinning a yarn that made the mouse vanish irretrievably.

Nelly's dad, of course, had his suspicions but said nothing.

True to Nelly's word, however, the next five days passed by undeniably rodent free. Nelly's mum's feet had dropped lower down the rungs of her breakfast stool, and by Saturday all talk of the mouse had generally been dropped.

Only Asti seemed morbidly keen to know more.

'Which bit did Barney swallow first?' she asked. 'Head or tail?'

'He ate it sideways,' said Nelly, with a crunch of her cornflakes.

'I think the less talk there is in this house of mice, the better,' said Nelly's dad, pouring his third cup of coffee. 'THAT mouse is gone and THAT is the end of it. In fact from today, all talk of mice in this house is forbidden. By order of Dad.'

Asti's mouth opened and then shut without a sound. Nelly filled hers with another spoonful of cornflakes.

'You're so masterful sometimes, Clifford,' said Nelly's mum, rewarding him with a Bourbon biscuit.

147

'Daaaddd,' purred Nelly, sensing an opportunity had just come her way.

Uh-huh?' said her dad, with a masterful dunk of his biscuit.

'As you're so masterful and as you're such a hero and as you're such a fantastically brilliant dad . . .'

'Yes?' murmured her dad, sensing that a web of something not very convenient was about to be spun around him.

'Will you give me a lift to Crabtree Farm tomorrow?'

The tip of Nelly's dad's biscuit fell limply into his coffee. 'What time?' he sighed.

'About a quarter to one,' smiled Nelly sweetly.

'Monsters again?' he murmured, fishing around in his coffee with the back of a teaspoon.

'Yup,' said Nelly. 'New ones too!'

'Any other requests?' he asked.

'You don't by any chance have a walking stick, do you?' asked Nelly.

7

By some freak of a chance Nelly's dad did have a walking stick. He had bought it in an umbrella shop five years earlier with the intention of becoming a rambler. But after getting lost in the woods on his first ramble, and limping home four hours after dark, he had hung, or rather propped up his stick once and for all.

For the last five years, his highly varnished *English Adventurer* walking stick had been retired to the furthermost corner of the shed.

Today, courtesy of Nelly and a J-cloth, it was cobweb-free and about to descend into the Crabtree marshes.

'Thanks for the lift, Dad,' said Nelly with a clunk of the passenger door.

'Can you pick me up from here at six, please?' she asked, tramping across the verge in

her wellingtons. 'I'll be waiting right here by the bridge.'

'Will do,' said her dad with a wave.

Nelly blew a kiss to him as he turned the car around in the farm entrance just beyond the bridge and then pointed the Maestro back in the direction of home.

'See you at six,' mouthed Nelly, closing her palm around the handle of her walking stick and then turning towards the river to survey the fields and marshes that lay on either side.

'Glad you could make it, Nelly,' echoed the voice of Claudius from somewhere in the vicinity of her wellingtons.

Nelly jumped. Where was the voice coming from? Her eyes darted to the moss-carpeted brickwork of the river bridge and then dived brick by brick to the verge. There was lots of grass but no Digdigg to be seen.

'Follow me!' echoed Claudius's voice again. 'My wife can't wait to meet you.'

Nelly scratched her head. There was still no Digdigg to be seen. She dropped down low to grass level with a frown and then stood up abruptly as a passing car sped towards the bridge in the direction of town. Keen not to appear suspicious to anyone passing by, she wrenched off one of her wellingtons, tipped it upside down and pretended to shake out an unwanted stone. The car sped by oblivious.

She replaced her wellington with a wobble and then crouched down low beside the bridge again. The grass was tangled and knotted like scarecrow hair, perfect cover for a Digdigg.

'I'm in here,' echoed Claudius, his pink, twitching nose emerging from the hole in an empty Fanta can. 'I see you found a walking stick!'

Nelly smiled as his head emerged from the can.

'Bit of a squeeze the holes in these tins,' he went on. 'I wish they'd make them a little bit bigger. Maybe my wife is right,' he winced, poking his paws out and clamping his claws down on either side of the hole. 'Maybe I have put on a bit of weight recently.'

'Can I help pull you out?' said Nelly, trying to be helpful.

'No, I can manage, thank you,' said Claudius determinedly. 'I might be strong and I might be tough and I might be fast and I might be secretive and I might be a little plumper around the midriff than I used to be, but I most definitely am not incapable.'

Nelly stood corrected and propped her walking stick up against the bridge.

'Are you sure you don't want me to help?' she smiled, trying not to laugh as Claudius's blue and white furry body began to squeeze out of the Fanta can like Playdoh from a play factory.

'Bingo!' he said, rolling out on to the grass and then springing to his feet.

'Welcome to Digdigg territory, Nelly!' he said, shinning up the ivy-clad wall of the road bridge and then directing Nelly's attention to the open fields with a broad sweep of his paw. 'I know every blade of sedge and every tractor furrow between here and the next bridge up.'

Nelly eyes switched from one side of the river to the other. To the right, higher ground lay to the east. This was working Crabtree Farm territory, where tractors had ploughed the fields into rich slabs of chocolate brown.

By way of contrast, the lower lying marshland to the west of the river was a pale and sedge-spiked green. Too boggy to plough and too treacherous to build houses on, it had remained untouched and undeveloped for centuries.

'I'll meet you at the bottom of the slope!' said Claudius, jumping from the bridge and then karate-chopping a nettle stalk with his paw.

Nelly took hold of her stick and prepared to inch her way through the waist-high carpet of faded nettles that lined the steep slope leading down from the bridge.

'The stingers must look like a rainforest to Claudius!' she thought, turning her wellington boots sideways and half stepping, half sliding down the slope.

At the bottom of the slope, stingers and dock gave way to marsh grass and squelch.

'Where's he gone?' thought Nelly, waiting for Claudius to reappear.

'We'll need to cross the fence soon,' he said, raising his head above the twiggy parapet of an empty blackbird's nest. 'Once we're inside the marsh, you must take extra care with every step.'

Nelly singled his red berry eyes out from the real berries of a hawthorn tree and then leaned inquisitively into the bush.

'How far away is your home?' she asked, throwing a glance at the distant railway line as a freight train rumbled through.

'Quite a way,' said Claudius with a twitch of his moustache.

Nelly peered skywards as Claudius climbed from the nest and scurried up the dagger-thorned branches to the very top of the tree. The hawthorn gave him a good view of the Crabtree Farm Estate both sides of the river.

With the balance and agility of a trapeze artist, he raised both paws to his forehead and peered long and hard across the marsh in the direction of Lowbridge town

'What are you looking for?' asked Nelly.

'Who, not what,' said Claudius, swivelling round 180 degrees to look across the river in the direction of Crabtree Farm.

'Who are you looking for?' asked Nelly, staring

up through the tangle of branches to the one remaining leaf on the tree.

'Jack Scab and his dog,' said Claudius. 'They come this way all too often for my liking. The two of them spell big trouble.'

With a final check of the landscape Claudius clambered down from the tree. 'All clear,' he said. 'Now follow me.'

8

'Who's Jack Scab?' said Nelly, turning the back of her Puffa jacket into the hawthorn spikes and reversing her way through and past the bush.

Claudius scurried to the top of a barbed wire fence post and closed his paws tightly into boxer's fists. 'Never met him, never want to,' he replied, swinging an imaginary left hook at the sky.

'Why not?' asked Nelly.

'As I said,' frowned Claudius with a perfectly executed right uppercut, 'Jack Scab is trouble. I've seen his work.'

From the way Claudius had bristled, Nelly decided she had better concentrate on the journey in hand and ask questions about Jack Scab later.

'This is where we enter the marsh, Nelly,' said Claudius, tightrope-walking along a strand of barbed wire to the next fence post and jumping down on the marsh side.

Nelly made her way to the post, stooped low, and then gingerly took hold of the uppermost strand of wire. Tight as a guitar string, spiky as a cactus, there was a distinct feeling of 'keep out' about this fence.

With as much poise as she could muster, she raised her first wellington awkwardly and lifted it over the lower strand.

'Oo-er!' gasped Nelly. Her front boot was already sinking fast!

With a twist and a bit of a stumble she eased the rest of her Puffa jacket through the gap and dragged her second wellington through.

'Follow the acorns, Nelly!' said Claudius, ducking out of sight into the sedge.

Nelly steadied herself with her walking stick and frowned. 'Follow the acorns? Follow what acorns?'

She looked down at her wellingtons and smiled.

Claudius had been busy. A bright green acorn had been stuck like a lollipop to a stick of dried sedge and pushed like a beacon into the ground.

'Mini signposts!' smiled Nelly, looking five metres further ahead, and then further on again. 'How clever!'

She was right. Claudius had been busy all week, in fact, plotting Nelly a hazard-free route across the marsh. The way the line of acorns snaked, turned and doubled back, it was clear that hidden pockets of treacherous ooze lay at every twist and turn.

'Too right I'll follow the acorns!' Nelly thought, stepping cautiously into the squelch.

It was heavy going. Even with the help of a safely plotted Digdigg line, the suck and ooze of the boggy terrain took its toll on her weary calves.

'Keep going,' smiled Claudius. 'My wife can't wait to meet you. We've been polishing our furniture all week!'

Nelly leaned on her walking stick and smiled. Polishing the furniture? That was a new one!

'What's your wife's name?' she asked, ploughing on through the bog.

'Nero,' said Claudius.

'That's a nice name,' coughed Nelly, trying to mask her surprise.

'We're going to cut right in a moment, Nelly,' said Claudius. 'Can you see that little mound of ground in the distance over there?'

Nelly took her eyeline from Claudius's outstretched paw, and squinted across a nondescript area of marshy nothing.

'Try looking from my height,' he went on, encouraging Nelly to stoop low.

'That could be difficult!' she laughed, doing her best to lower her sights to Digdigg height without soggying her knees.

Claudius pointed again. 'We live in the middle of the marsh over there – can you see? Where the ground rises ever so slightly.'

Nelly was far too tall to see. Even at her lowest crouch level, she had no idea where Claudius was

pointing. There was nothing else for it. Laying her stick on the ground, she lowered herself into the soft wet stubble of the marsh and placed her body into a press-up position.

Marsh ooze bubbled round her wrists and the toes of her wellingtons slid out of sight as she turned one cheek and peered across the horizon.

'I can see it!' she smiled. 'There IS a little mound, just where you said.'

Claudius lined his eyes up alongside hers, and nodded.

'That's where we live, Nelly. Quite a secret, eh!'

'No wonder no one knows you live here!' said Nelly, lifting herself from the floor and wiping her hands on the sleeves of her coat.

'No one ever comes here!' laughed Claudius. 'That helps!'

'Except Jack Scab?' asked Nelly inquisitively.

Claudius's blue and white furry hackles rose again, and his paws closed into fists.

'Let's continue our journey,' he said, 'and I will tell you about Jack Scab.'

9

'Jack Scab is a poacher. An evil, sadistic animal trapper,' scowled Claudius. 'He skulks around these parts with his hellhound of a dog, looking for animals to catch and fur to rip from their backs.'

'You mean he skins the animals he catches?' asked Nelly, squelching her way around an S-bend of acorns.

'Skins them alive,' said Claudius, his knuckles turning white.

Nelly gasped. 'And then what does he do with them?' she asked.

'He feeds them to his dog Satan, the most bloodthirsty, bone-breaking, sinew-snapping beast that ever wagged a tail.'

'I meant, what does he do with the furs?' said Nelly, stumbling slightly as she conjured with the horror of it all.

'He sews them into patchwork bed quilts,' shuddered Claudius, 'and sells them to Antarctica.'

'Antarctica?' said Nelly. 'I thought they had loads of fur in Antarctica!'

'Not water vole,' said Claudius. 'Not English water vole especially.'

Nelly stumbled again and then stared across the marsh towards the river. 'I didn't know there were water voles on the river.'

'There aren't any more,' said Claudius. 'Jack Scab's skinned them all. And the red squirrels. The Crabtree woods used to be full of red squirrels.'

'Red squirrels!' gasped Nelly. 'I thought you only found red squirrels in Scotland!'

'You do now,' said Claudius, 'thanks to him.'

'That's terrible!' gasped Nelly.

'It's worse than terrible,' said Claudius, punching his way through the sedge. 'Water vole, red squirrel, grey squirrel, fox, mink, rat, rabbit, field mouse, stoat, weasel, badger . . .'

'Badger!' gasped Nelly.

'Oh yes,' said Claudius, 'Jack Scab traps and

skins the lot. The more animal varieties he can sew into his patchwork, the more money his novelty quilts can command. They'll pay a pretty price in Antarctica for a patchwork quilt that includes English badger.'

Nelly snaked her way past the next slalom of acorns in silence, trying to decide which question she dare ask next.

'But how does he sell them to Antarctica?'

'Something called an internet,' said Claudius. 'Apparently you can buy and sell just about anything if you've got yourself an internet. Never mind if it's illegal.'

Nelly nodded. She'd pretty much heard the same.

'What breed of dog is it?' she asked.

'The worst kind,' said Claudius. 'The word on the marsh is that Scab's dog is an ungodly cross between a Dobermann, a Rottweiler, a bloodhound, an American pitbull, a lurcher, a greyhound and a Jack Russell.'

'That does sound like trouble,' shuddered Nelly.

'Vicious, fast, aggressive, greedy – it's

everything you don't want a dog to be, and more,' Claudius expanded.

'More?' thought Nelly. 'How could there be more?'

'It's blind in both eyes too,' explained Claudius. 'The word among the farm animals is that Scab blinded his dog at birth to develop its sense of smell.'

Nelly stopped dead in her tracks and stared open-jawed at her feet.

'That's how it hunts,' said Claudius, placing his paw on the toe of her wellington. 'Not by sight, but by smell. It could sniff out a weasel's cough from five acres.'

Nelly steadied herself on her walking stick for a moment, more from shock than fatigue.

A bracing trek across the marsh had suddenly taken on a rather darker dimension. What if Jack Scab was lurking in their vicinity now? What if Satan picked up on their scent? How much would the Antarcticans pay for a furry patchwork quilt that included the blue and white stripe of a Digdigg?

Nelly and Claudius set off again in silence, but it was no good – she had to ask the question.

'What if Scab's dog picks up on your scent, Claudius?' she wavered. 'Isn't it too dangerous for you to be out on the marsh at all?'

Claudius smiled up at her appreciatively. 'Digdiggs have no scent, Nelly. We leave no trail in the air, whichever way the wind is blowing.'

That, as far as Nelly was concerned, was the best news she had heard all day. The beat of her heart steadied a little, but then her eyebrows arched with concern.

'But what about me?' she asked. 'Say Satan picked up on my scent, wouldn't he come hunting for me?'

'Not a chance,' laughed Claudius, 'unless you're furrier than you look! Satan has no interest in you, and neither does Jack Scab. He's a loner. He keeps his evil business private and he stays well away from people and the town.'

Nelly flash-framed every visit she'd ever made to town through her mind. She couldn't recall ever seeing anyone fitting Jack Scab's description in Lowbridge. Not in the high street or the precinct, or on her route home from school, or even as far away as the canal. From the sound of him, she would be perfectly happy if it stayed that way.

'Now then,' said Claudius, 'that's enough about Jack Scab. Come and say hello to my family, Nelly. This, my friend, is our home!'

10

Nelly's wellies ground to a surprise halt. She had been so engrossed in the horrors of Jack Scab and his dog, she hadn't noticed how far they had walked. She was standing in the middle of the marsh now, perhaps twenty-five minutes' trudge from the road.

'I had no idea we had come so far!' she said, peering back towards the far-distant Crabtree Bridge. 'And you're right!' she exclaimed, staring down at her feet. 'The ground IS higher here!'

Claudius hopped from the toe of her wellington and placed his paw around a plaited loop of sedge that speared upwards from the right of the mound.

'Everyone will be so pleased to meet you,' he said, tugging the loop sharply three times.

Nelly fixed her eyes on the ground and then

stepped back as the ground began to move. A low
sludging rasp belched from the marsh and a
metre-square turf of wet sedge slowly began to
rise before her.

'It's a trapdoor!' she beamed excitedly. 'I knew
it would be! It's a trapdoor beneath the marsh!'

As the square of sedge lifted further, a golden
sliver of honeyed light sprang up from the void
below. As the trapdoor opened wider, six

concrete steps yawned into view.

'After you, Nelly!' said Claudius, with a welcoming sweep of his paw.

Nelly peered down into the hole. She had imagined the Digdiggs' home would be grey and a little uninviting, but the cosy glow that beckoned beneath her had her wondering.

'It will be a bit smaller than you're used to,' smiled Claudius. 'Just two modest rooms, I'm afraid. And mind your head as you go through to meet my wife. The doorway is a little low.'

'Not too low for a Digdigg, I hope!' laughed Nelly, lowering her wellington on to the first concrete step. 'If it's too low for a Digdigg then it'll be far too low for a Nelly!'

Claudius chuckled. 'Air raid shelters weren't built for Digdiggs, Nelly. They were built for humans. If you look where you're going, you'll be fine!'

Nelly dropped down deeper into the warm buttery light of the Digdiggs' underground home. The hole she was stepping into was just about wide enough for her shoulders to squeeze through, making last-minute scrunchy adjustments awkward to say the least.

'I'll follow you down,' said Claudius as Nelly's head dropped below his knees. 'Remember, my wife's name is Nero!'

Nelly nodded, and dropped her head below ground level. To her right, at the base of one grey wall, a line of birthday-sized candles were flickering like miniature torches. Directly ahead of her, a low rectangular doorway was glowing golden like the entrance to an Egyptian tomb.

'OK, kids, you can close the hatch now,' said Claudius, hopping down the concrete steps and signalling to his children with a wave of his paw.

Nelly stiffened.

To her left . . . to her immediate left . . . almost within touching distance of her arm . . . something huge and momentous was moving.

Nelly swallowed drily, gripped the knob of her walking stick and dragged her eyes towards it.

'What the . . .' she gasped.

There in the flickering shadows directly beside her, and spanning almost the entire length of one concrete wall, a giant wire-framed wheel was turning – or rather being turned, by the scribbling scrabbling paws of one hundred and twenty Digdigg children.

'It's like a giant hamster wheel!' Nelly gulped, her gaze tumbling to the bottom of the wheel, where a miniature stampede of blue and white furry bodies were thundering like little athletes on a treadmill.

'Ingenious, eh?' said Claudius, scampering towards the wheel. 'Designed and made it myself,' he swaggered.

Nelly was all eyes and no words.

'I picked up all the little pieces of wire when they were erecting the fence along the marsh,' explained Claudius, keen to impart his full genius. 'The fence builders just dropped them on the ground, so I put them all to good use!'

Nelly nodded slowly. She'd never seen anything like it.

'The wheel is attached to these ropes and pulleys,' Claudius continued, with an upwards sweep of his paw, 'and the ropes and pulleys are attached to the trapdoor, see? This is how we open and close it.'

'Is that your . . . ?'

'Doorbell, yes,' interrupted Claudius, sweeping his whiskery snout in the direction of a cat bell and collar attached to a long swooping thread of woven vine. 'I found that too,' he boasted. 'Bit of a job dragging it home across the fields, but it certainly does the job.'

Nelly peered low at the small silver cat bell. It was hanging from a pink diamante collar, and had been attached to the wall with a bent masonry nail.

'Remember, three tugs for entry, Nelly,' Claudius smiled, pinging the small circular bell with his claw. 'Any more or any less and the hatch stays shut.'

Nelly was speechless. She had no idea that a space as ordinary as a concrete underground air raid shelter could conceal so many surprises!

'Come on,' laughed Claudius as the trapdoor closed above their heads. 'I must introduce you to Nero. Please follow me through to the lounge.'

Nelly closed her mouth and looked back at the giant hamster wheel.

One by one the Digdigg children were releasing their grip on the wire rungs of the wheel and flopping with high-pitched squeaks into a tumble of whiskers and paws. Bouncing like bingo balls on to the floor, they began to gather in numbers around the soles of Nelly's wellies.

'Whoa! Don't tread on them!' thought Nelly, hardly daring to lift her wellingtons from the floor.

'Are you Nelly the Monster Sitter? Are you Nelly the Monster Sitter?' chorused the multitude of mini Digdiggs now crowding around her boots.

'Yes I am,' said Nelly.

'Come and meet our mother! Come and meet our mother!' squeaked the carpet of blue and white giggles.

'I'd love to meet your mum!' laughed Nelly, turning towards the lounge, hitting her forehead on the concrete lintel and blacking out.

11

When Nelly came to, she thought she'd died and gone to heaven.

'Where am I?' she swooned, lifting her cheek from the floor and blinking through a golden blur of shimmer and sparkle.

'In our lounge,' said an out-of-focus Claudius. 'Well, one half of you is in the lounge – your legs are still in the lobby.'

'How long have I been out?' Nelly groaned.

'About fifteen minutes,' said Claudius.

Nelly dragged herself up from the floor and leaned her back against the concrete of the door frame. With a woozy shake of her head, she squinted into the golden dazzle that filled the room. Boy, had Nero been polishing!

'Ouch!' she winced, with a prod of her index finger. She had a bump on her forehead the size of an egg.

'I didn't squash anyone when I fell, did I?' she gasped.

'No,' laughed a dazzling but blurry Claudius. 'As I said before, we Digdiggs can put on a bit of a spurt when we need to!'

Nelly inched herself up the door frame a little more, and gazed groggily at the candlelit floor of the Digdiggs' lounge. Everywhere she tried to focus, sparkle sparkled back. There was sparkle at her fingertips, shimmer at the foot of each welly, and dazzle in all of the glittering areas in between.

'Are you feeling OK, Nelly? Would you like me to take you home?' asked Claudius.

'I'll be fine, thanks, Claudius,' she swooned, rubbing her eyes. 'Just give me a moment to get my bearings.'

There weren't many bearings to get. Nelly was sitting on the floor of an underground air raid shelter that was no bigger than four metres square. She had travelled approximately two metres from the concrete bottom step, hit her head on the concrete lintel, and fallen to the concrete floor, directly in front of the concrete entrance to the concrete lounge.

'Concrete hurts!' she said, cupping her hand over the bump on her forehead.

'Are you sure you're all right, Miss Monster Sitter?' said an unfamiliar voice. 'My husband will gladly take you home if you wish.'

Nelly looked down. Close to the outstretched fingers of her right hand, a second adult Digdigg had stepped into blurry view. She was similar in proportion to Claudius, but had a lipstick-red moustache, snowberry-white eyes and plaits of braided blue fur.

'You must be Nero,' Nelly smiled, extending her little finger for a handshake.

'That's right,' smiled Claudius's wife, stepping forward and placing both paws warmly around the tip of Nelly's fingernail. 'And you must be Nelly the Monster Sitter.'

'Nelly the Concrete Hitter, more like!' smiled Nelly, gently rubbing the bump on her head. 'Please, everyone call me Nelly.'

'HELLO, NELLLLLLLLY!' chorused one hundred and twenty Digdiggs.

Although the entire Digdigg family only had eyes for Nelly, Nelly found her own eyes drawn irresistibly back to the floor. What was it with this room? Where was the dazzle coming from?

She rubbed her eyes again and did a double take.

She rubbed her eyes twice more.

It wasn't an air raid shelter. It was a palace!

The floor beneath her wasn't concrete grey at all, it was carpeted from corner to corner with a mosaic of circular golden tiles. Even more extravagantly, along the base of every wall, glitter and sparkle spilled upwards like the crimped edge of a huge golden pie crust.

Nelly swept her fingers curiously across the brightly polished surface of the floor beneath her, and then slid down on to one elbow for an extra-close-up look.

On closer inspection each circular golden floor tile seemed to be imprinted with its own individual design: an eagle, a lion, a griffin, an emperor's head . . .

AN EMPEROR'S HEAD?

Nelly frowned and then squeaked. These weren't circular tiles at all – they were Roman coins! Her eyes flashed to the edges of the room. Never mind golden pie crusts, they were golden plates!

'Where did you find these?' she gasped, skimming the palm of her hand across the floor like a curling stone. 'And those!' she said, pointing to the glittering plates and salvers that were propped up against each wall.

'In the fields,' said Claudius with a shrug. 'The Crabtree Farm tractors used to plough them up and I used to dig them out.'

'Do you know what these are?' gasped Nelly.

'I know you can't eat them!' said Claudius, grinning like a Cheshire cat to reveal the absence of two front teeth.

'Do you like the effect they give?' asked Nero. 'I wasn't sure at first whether they worked with the candles or not.'

Nelly nodded slowly, staring goldstruck around the room.

'Enough about boring old floor coverings,' said Claudius with a clap of his paws. 'Let's not forget why we asked Nelly over here in the first place!'

Nelly lifted her eyes from the mosaic of golden coins and focused on Claudius. Claudius had slipped his paw around his wife's waist and had drawn her towards him excitedly.

'Nero and I can have our very first trip together to the PRECINCT!'

Nelly smiled and moved into a cross-legged position. She had decided not to stand up in the presence of any Digdiggs; not only was she able to focus on them more clearly, there was also next to no chance of her hitting her head on a concrete doorway again!

'So that's why you've asked me to monster sit!' she chuckled. 'You fancy a trip to the precinct, do you? I'm sure I could suggest some more romantic places to go than that!'

Claudius raised his paw. 'It isn't romance we're

looking for, Nelly, it's something much more enchanting than that.'

Nero slipped her paw through her husband's arm. 'Ever since I've been with child,' she said, patting her tummy lightly with her paw, 'Claudius has been getting cravings.'

Claudius nodded. 'I always get them when there's a baby on the way.'

Nelly tried her best not to frown. She was sure it was pregnant mums who were meant to get cravings, not expectant dads.

Claudius licked his lips and then drew his wife closer to his side. 'Do you know what I could eat right now?' he drooled. 'Do you know what Nero and I are going to try for the first time this afternoon?'

Nelly scratched her head. If it came from the precinct, it couldn't be that enchanting.

'A doner kebab!' drooled Claudius.

'A doner kebab!' echoed Nero.

'A DONER KEBABBBBB!!!!!' chorused the children.

Nelly did her best not to shudder.

'Do you know what's actually IN a doner kebab?' she asked.

'Nope,' said Claudius, 'but I've smelled them. Boy, have I smelled them. They smell diiiiiiviiiiiiiiiiiiiiine!'

'The rats in the precinct kebab shop say doner kebabs are to die for, don't they, Claudius?' said Nero.

Claudius nodded. 'That's right. I caught up with a bunch of them last time I was in town. The rats from the kebab shop say once you've tried a doner kebab, you'll never look at a sack of corn again.'

Nelly folded and then unfolded her arms. 'But how are you going to buy a doner kebab? They only do them in medium and large sizes.'

Claudius twitched his moustache and then broke out into a fit of giggles.

'Buy? BUY? Digdiggs don't buy things! We forage for things! We scout around, we use our bonces. Digdiggs don't have any money to buy things. All we have are the contents of this room!'

Nelly cast her eye over the carpet of Roman

gold, but decided not to go there.

'The rats told Claudius that there's a hole that leads beneath the drainpipe of the precinct building,' said Nero excitedly. 'It leads into the kebab shop, through the pitta bread cupboard and right under the shop counter,' she beamed. 'The rats told Claudius that sometimes when the men are carving the meat, they drop bits on the floor, and if you're REALLY QUICK you can grab a piece before they pick them up and put them back into the pitta bread!'

Nelly turned pale at the thought. The one and only doner kebab she'd ever eaten had come from that selfsame shop in the precinct.

'Nero and I have never been able to venture anywhere outside our home together before,' said Claudius. 'One of us has always had to remain behind, to look after the children.'

'Well, you'd better get moving the two of you then,' she said, 'or at this rate it will be time for me to leave before you're even halfway across the marsh!'

'We'll be off then!' squeaked Nero, linking

arms with her husband and blowing a round of kisses to all of their children.

'Stay put, kids!' said Nelly, clambering to her feet and then paying extra care as she ducked through the concrete doorway into the lobby. 'It's my turn to spin the wheel!'

The Digdigg children remained obediently in the lounge as their mother and father scuttled into the lobby.

'Bye, kids!' said Claudius. 'Be good for Nelly!'

'WE WILLLLLLLLLL!!!!!!!' came a one-hundred-and-twenty-strong reply.

With a scurry and six hops, Claudius and Nero were at the top of the concrete stairs.

'See you around five, Nelly,' squeaked Nero as a sliver of afternoon daylight splintered downwards into the lobby from the marshland above. 'That will give you plenty of time to walk back to the bridge.'

'Shall we bring you back some kebab?' said Claudius, with a twiddle of his freshly waxed moustache.

'No thank you,' Nelly laughed, waving them

both on their way 'I'll have a Sunday roast with all the trimmings waiting for me when I get home. My mum's a brilliant cook!' she fibbed.

With a parting wave Nero and Claudius darted through the narrow crack of light that Nelly's perfect wheel rotation had produced. With a twang of their curly tails they were gone.

'OK, kids,' smiled Nelly, sealing the hatch and turning back to the lounge. 'Let the games commence!'

12

Nelly had never monster sat one hundred and twenty children all at once before, and she was relieved when she returned to the lounge to find them all sitting obediently on their stools.

'Hello everybody,' she smiled, resuming her cross-legged position across the doorway.

'HeelllllllOOO!' chorused her little furry audience.

There were four long arcing rows of thirty

stools each, arranged in the style of a cinema circle. 'They're certainly very shiny!' said Nelly, placing the palms of her hands on the floor and running her eyes across each row in turn. 'Has your mum been polishing them?'

'We all have,' chorused the children. 'We like polishing!'

'Good job too!' thought Nelly. 'You'd need to like polishing if you lived in a place like this!'

'Now then,' Nelly faltered, 'how am I going to remember all of your names?'

'Our names are on top of our stools!' squeaked one of the older children from the centre of the back row. 'My name's Hadrian – see?' he squeaked, slipping from his stool and pointing to the top of his seat. 'See? It says "Hadrian" in writing just here!'

Nelly lowered her head for a closer inspection of each glittering stool. In true Digdigg style, each was constructed from a pile of golden coins – a one-coin stack for the youngest and smallest children, a ten-coin stack for the tallest and eldest.

'Did your daddy make these?' she asked.

'Yes,' replied Hadrian. 'Every birthday he glues another shiny disc on top.'

'That makes you ten!' she said, counting her way upwards from the floor to a glittering coin from the reign of Emperor Hadrian, dated AD 132. 'And you're right,' she smiled, 'there is your name on top!'

'My name's Titus and I'm four,' squeaked one of the younger Digdiggs from the second row.'

'My name is Vitellius and I'm six,' squeaked a pigtailed Digdigg from a slightly higher stool in Row Three.

Nelly's eyes frog-hopped from stool to stool and from Emperor's head to Emperor's head. Trajan, Domitian Vespasian, Nerva, Macrinus, Seleucus, Gordian the First, Gordian the Second – the entire history of the Roman Empire was set out before her in Roman coins!

'Well, my name is Nelly and it's time to play some games!' she laughed, crawling backwards towards the doorway and crossing her legs again.

'Now then, what would you like to play?'

'POLISSSSHHHHIIINNNNNGGGG!!!!!'
cheered the Digdiggs in a frenzy of excitement.

Nelly shook her head. POLISHING? 'We are
not playing polishing!' she laughed.

The happy smiles slipped from the furry faces
of Nelly's audience, and one by one each of the
little Digdiggs lowered its head with a frown.

'No one plays polishing . . .' exclaimed Nelly,
'. . . do they?'

'We do,' squeaked Piso, from a two-coin stool
to the far right of Row One.

Nelly scooted across the glittering floor on her
bottom, and parked herself directly in front of
her audience. 'Surely there must be some other
games that Digdiggs like to play?'

Piso's mouth opened and then shut without
a word.

'Trajan?' said Nelly, leaning to her left to
glean another name from the top of a six-coin
golden stool. 'What other kind of games do you
like to play?'

Trajan looked at his brothers and sisters, and
then frowned.

'We only like playing polishing,' he said. 'Polishing is fun!'

Nelly looked at her watch. It had just gone two o'clock. Surely she wasn't going to spend the next three hours polishing?

She thought for a moment and then slapped her thigh. 'What about Musical Chairs?' she said. 'Musical Chairs is perfect – we've got a hundred and twenty stools to play with, and we can use the ringtone on my mobile phone for the music. Shall I tell you how to play Musical Chairs?'

One hundred and twenty pairs of Digdigg ears listened carefully to Nelly's explanation of how to play Musical Chairs and then one hundred and twenty Digdigg heads shook solemnly.

'Polish the Chairs would be all right,' said Heraclonus, from the middle of the second row.

Nelly sat in silence for a moment and racked her brains. But whenever she lifted her head with a smile, the Digdiggs dropped theirs with a frown.

They were polish obsessed!

When Nelly suggested I Spy, they suggested I Polish.

When Nelly suggested Simon Says, they suggested Simon Says Polish.

By the time Murder in the Dark became Polish in the Dark, Nelly was clean out of ideas.

'Give me a moment,' she faltered, glancing at her watch again. She would think of something to play if it took all afternoon.

Her Digdigg audience waited with bated breath, whiskers bristling and eyes twinkling.

'Howzabout . . .' murmured Nelly. 'Howzabout if I teach you . . . SOME SONGS TO SING WHEN YOU'RE POLISHING?'

It was the best idea she could think of. And to her total delight and relief, it appeared to be an idea that was very well received!

Nelly smiled. At last she had struck gold with an idea. She sat up straight, waited for the hubbub to hush, and then waved her right hand like a conductor's baton.

'OK, here we go. One, two, three . . . One hundred and twenty bottles of polish,' she sang, 'hanging on the wall. One hundred and twenty bottles of polish hanging on the wall. Come on, everyone,' she beckoned, 'join in! . . . And if one bottle of polish should accidently fall, there'd be one hundred and nineteen bottles of polish hanging on the wall!'

After five verses, Rows Three and Four had caught on. By Verse Eight, Row Two was in full swing and by Verse Fourteen even the tiniest of the tiny Digdiggs was in full squeak.

'Only one hundred and five verses to go!' groaned Nelly, waving her imaginary baton.

Backwards and forwards her furry audience rocked.

'Clap your paws!' shouted Nelly as they moved up to Verse Twenty-five.

'Tap your toes!' she shouted as the fiftieth bottle of polish accidentally fell.

By the time there were no more bottles of polish hanging on the wall, the walls of the lounge and lobby were resounding like a cathedral, and Nelly's voice was as hoarse as a frog.

She raised her arms like a schoolteacher and brought the children to order.

'No more!' she gasped. 'It's taken over half an hour to sing one song!'

'MORRRRE!!!' chorused the children, waving their little furry arms in the air.

'I don't know any more!' croaked Nelly, certain that her voice couldn't hold out for one hundred and twenty verses of another song.

'MORRRRE, NELLY – MORRRE!!!' the Digdigg children squeaked. 'SING US ANOTHER POLISHING SONG!!'

Nelly puffed out her cheeks. 'All right,' she sighed. 'I suppose I could think of another song we can sing.'

Nelly cleared her throat and raised her imaginary baton again.

'One man went to polish . . . went to polish a meadow. One man and his duster . . . squeak squeak! . . . went to polish a meadow!!'

The Digdigg children looked at each other and then waited for the second verse to unfold.

Nelly ploughed on.

'Two men went to polish,' she croaked, 'went to polish a meadow. Two men, one man and their dusters . . . squeak squeak . . . went to polish a meadow.'

'Three men went to polish!' squeaked Titus.

After three verses one Digdigg voice had swelled to five.

After four verses five voices had swelled to twenty.

After ten minutes, twenty voices had swelled to eighty, and after twenty-five minutes, the concrete rafters were rocking again.

'They're a total bunch of nutters!' thought Nelly.

13

'Enough!' chuckled Nelly, pretending to throw her imaginary baton over her shoulder, as the one hundred and twentieth man polished his very last meadow.

'Enough, I say! No more polishing meadows! No more polishing anything at all!' she groaned.

Four rows of little Digdiggs collapsed in a fit of giggles. It had taken nearly forty minutes to sing that song!

'Nelly,' said Olympius, climbing back on to his stool. 'What sort of things do you polish in the house where you live?'

All the other Digdigg children took their cue from Olympius and clambered on to their stools too.

Nelly furrowed her brow. 'My school shoes. That's about it really.'

One hundred and twenty inquisitive paws sprang into the air all at once. Nelly groaned and braced herself for the longest question-and-answer session of her life.

1.   No, she didn't study polish at school.

2.   No, she didn't ask for polish for her birthday.

3.   Yes, she did know how to spell polish.

4.   No, she didn't know how to make polish.

. . .

21. No, she didn't know who invented polish.

. . .

36. No, she didn't think anyone polished the sun.

37. Yes, she did know the sun had the biggest shine.

. . .

48. No, her parents didn't polish as much as the Digdiggs' parents.

. . .

59. No, her sister didn't polish anything ever at all.

66. No, if she had three wishes she wouldn't

wish for three lots of polish.

89. No, she didn't know any stories about polish.

93. No, she had never dreamt she was a duster.

118. No, she had never wanted to jump into a bath full of polish.

. . .

120. And no no no no no, if she had a pet beetle, no, she wouldn't call it Polish or even Shiny!

Nelly pulled her scrunchy from her ponytail and shook her long liquorice-black hair free. What was it with Digdiggs and polish?

She looked at her watch and gasped. It was half past four already! Claudius and Nero would be due home before long, and she had spent almost the entire afternoon singing about POLISH.

She could feel the threat of a migraine coming on. With a soothing rub of her temples, she slid her scrunchy back into place.

'I know,' she smiled. 'Howzabout I ask *you* some questions for a change?'

'GOOD IDEA!!!!' chorused the Digdiggs.

Nelly rocked thoughtfully backwards and forwards, stroking her chin with her fingers.

'Now then,' she mused, 'what question shall I ask you all first?'

All four rows of Digdiggs leaned forward on their stools, eager to be the first to provide the answer.

'I know!' said Nelly, leaning back with a smile, but then straightening her back with a jolt.

All eyes flashed to the cat bell. The Digdiggs' doorbell was ringing, only not three times as agreed. It was jangling and rattling and vibrating and shaking like it had never done before.

'Something's wrong!' thought Nelly, leaping to her feet and wheeling through the doorway into the lobby. 'Stay there, children,' she cried.

Stabbing her fingers between the wire rungs of the wheel she motioned to turn the hatch pulleys into action. And then stopped.

Claudius's orders had been quite precise. 'Any more than three rings, any less than three rings, and the hatch must stay closed!'

Nelly's heart jackhammered. The cat bell was out of control, shaking and trembling with so much force it was working itself loose from the collar!

'I've got to risk it!' gasped Nelly, wrenching the wheel into motion and staring at the roof hatch with her heart in her mouth.

The instant the hatch of the underground shelter lifted, Nero tumbled through. She fell with a bump on to the top concrete step and rolled perilously close to the edge.

'Nero!' cried Nelly, glancing anxiously at the shaft of light that had pierced the lobby from the marshland above. 'Where's Claudius?'

Nero lay panting breathlessly on the step, her white berry eyes transparent with fear. She had been running and running fast, and her soft downy bosom was empty of air. One hundred and twenty frightened pairs of eyes gathered around Nelly's wellingtons as Nero finally mustered the strength to raise her head and speak.

'Jack Scab!' she gasped with terror-torn eyes. 'Claudius has been captured by Jack Scab!'

14

Nelly lifted Nero from the step and carried her gently through to the lounge.

'Close the hatch quickly, children,' she said, cupping Nero in both palms. 'Nero,' she whispered, 'you must tell me what has happened!'

Nelly watched anxiously as Nero's eyelids fluttered open weakly. The soft downy fur of her cheeks was furrowed with tears.

'We were making our way home from town,' she sobbed. 'We had cut beneath the railway line, and crossed the main road safely,' she sobbed, 'when . . .'

Nelly looked down. The children had closed the hatch and gathered anxiously in the lounge doorway. Conscious that they might hear something that would distress them even more, Nelly lifted Nero's body to eye level.

'When what?' she whispered softly.

Nero swallowed drily and continued with her story.

'When Claudius spotted a pile of rubbish that had been dumped near the Bitter Avenue layby, in the trees behind, on the edge of the marsh. People are always dumping things there. It's one of Claudius's favourite places to visit,' she sobbed. 'He's always on the hunt for something he can use.'

Nelly knew the exact spot that Nero was referring to. It was a thicket of daylight–starved trees surrounding a shallow and rubbish-filled pond. So many fly-tippers had been using the screen of trees to conceal their illegal dumping that the problem had been the subject of a recent local TV report.

'We'd had a wonderful time in town,' sobbed Nero. 'We'd had our first delicious taste of kebab, we'd made friends with some perfectly charming rats . . . everything was perfect . . . until . . .'

'Until what?' whispered Nelly, trying her best to get the full picture from Nero as quickly as she possibly could.

'Until we crawled into the first rubbish bag,' sobbed Nero, her shoulders beginning to shake uncontrollably. 'It was horrible! It was terrible! He just came from nowhere!'

'Who did?' whispered Nelly. 'Jack Scab?'

'No, that awful dog of his,' convulsed Nero. 'It poked its snout right into the middle of the bag between us. I could smell the blood on its breath, Nelly!'

Nelly's eyes widened.

'It must have picked up on our scent,' sobbed Nero.

Nelly nodded ruefully and then shook her head.

'But Claudius said you don't carry any scent.'

'Chilli sauce,' sobbed Nero. 'We had doner kebab with extra chilli sauce. It was so delicious we couldn't help it. We got it all over our paws and down our fronts. We just weren't thinking.'

Nelly's head began to pound. This was as serious as monster sitting got.

'Nero, you have to tell me,' she whispered. 'Is Claudius . . . you know . . .'

Nelly looked painfully into Nero's eyes, expecting the very worst.

Nero lifted her shoulders and dropped them like dead weight.

'I'm not sure. I just don't know,' she sobbed. 'All I know is that Claudius grabbed hold of the dog's whiskers and told me to run. So I did. Straight through Jack Scab's legs. The last I saw of Claudius was as I looked back. He was crawling into the open neck of a pink plastic can. I hope against hope he's still in there now.'

Nelly did her best to picture the awful scene. 'A pink can, you say. Big or small?'

'Big,' sobbed Nero. 'It had a picture of a candle flame on the outside.'

'A paraffin can,' Nelly guessed. 'You definitely saw Claudius crawl inside?' she pressed.

Nero nodded her head grimly.

'Then he could still be alive!' whispered Nelly.

'If Scab's dog hasn't swallowed the can whole,' shuddered Nero. 'You should see its jaws, Nelly! You should smell its breath!'

Nelly raised her eyes towards the marsh.

It seemed unlikely that Scab's dog would swallow a paraffin can, however hungry it was. That meant Claudius was possibly alive. If he had managed to squeeze into the can then he might just have had a chance.

'Did Jack Scab see you?' continued Nelly.

'I don't think so,' sobbed Nero.

'Nero,' she asked, 'how long would Scab's dog be able to pick up on the scent of doner kebab with extra chilli sauce? How long would a scent like that remain in the air?'

'A few hours normally,' sobbed Nero, 'but for a dog with an unholy sense of smell, maybe as long as a day,' she shuddered. 'It depends.'

'Depends on what?' whispered Nelly.

'The strength of the wind and its direction,' trembled Nero.

'But what if Scab and his dog had picked up on your scent, Nero! Couldn't your scent have led them straight to our door?'

'I had to take that chance,' sobbed Nero. 'When I reached the marsh, the wind was blowing towards the town – the opposite direction to our home. I just had to take the chance.'

The more Nelly thought the dangers through, the worse they seemed to be. She logged the wind in her mind as a light easterly, and then pressed Nero for more much-needed information.

'So if Claudius gets free, he could run home without his scent being tracked?' she went on.

'It's possible,' blubbed Nero. 'Unless the wind changes direction while he's on the marsh.'

Nelly's face fell again. Another tripwire. If the wind changed to a westerly, Claudius wouldn't be able to run home at all. The risk of leading Scab's dog to his home and family would be too great. But if he ran in any other direction, Scab's dog would track him down for sure.

One thing was crystal clear. If Claudius was alive, Nelly had to do whatever she could do to save him from the jaws of Satan and the knife of Scab.

She needed to think quickly and, even more importantly, she needed to reach Claudius quickly! That would mean a direct route across the marsh to the Bitter Avenue bypass, with no acorns or Claudius to guide the way. Nero was in no fit state to lead her – besides, her place was at home with the children.

Nelly would be on her own on this one. She would have to face the dangers of the marsh with nothing but her walking stick and the bump on her head.

She needed a plan to free Claudius.

She needed a plan that would lead Scab and his dog right away from the marsh.

She needed a plan that would keep them away from the marsh for up to twenty-four hours.

And she needed a contingency plan that would work if the wind changed direction.

That was a lot of plans. A lot of plans she just didn't have.

Nelly put Nero down on the floor with her

children and looked anxiously at the crowd of tearful Digdiggs that had gathered mournfully around her wellingtons.

'How am I going to look after one hundred and twenty-one children on my own?' sobbed Nero caressing her pregnant belly.

'It won't come to that,' whispered Nelly. 'I won't let it come to that,' she insisted.

'Come on, plans! Where are you?' she agonized. 'How on earth am I going to approach a man like Scab? Scab the animal slaughterer. Scab the dog-blinder.'

Gong anywhere near a man like that was madness. Total madness.

. . .

Total madness?

. . .

Nelly stroked the bump on her forehead.

'Open the hatch, kids, I'm going out. Hadrian, I need to borrow your stool!'

15

Nelly's first thought when she set off from the mound was to wash off all traces of the chilli sauce scent from her wellingtons and hands. Using the ooze of the marsh like carbolic soap, she scrubbed them as though the future of the planet depended on it.

Barely half a kilometre further on, her only thought was of survival.

Crossing the marsh without Claudius was like trying to walk through one of her mum's cold moussakas. With a lung-busting groan she plunged the tip of her walking stick into the marsh and then toppled over as it sank into the bog.

'Not again,' she panted, as a cold creeping ooze seeped through her jeans. 'Mum's going to love me when I put these in the wash!'

Refusing to be beaten, she rose like a swamp monster and strode wearily on in the direction of Bitter Avenue.

Along with her walking stick Nelly was clinging to the fact that she had never heard any reports of anyone disappearing on the marsh. Surely then, she hoped and prayed, the chances of her being sucked down into the bowels of the earth were slim.

Anyway, this wasn't about her, it was about

Claudius. It was about reuniting a monster dad with the monster family who needed him. If she went in up to the bump on her forehead, so be it!

After five more lung-sapping minutes, her legs had turned to jelly and her calves had turned to stone. She could see the tatter of trees that screened the fly-tipping point on the distant horizon and took heart from the fact that her destination was in sight.

Three more hamstring-wrenching strides and she was flat on her face again. With a heave and a sludging rasp, she pulled her left wellington free from the ooze and staggered roadwards again.

Thoughts of Claudius, and Claudius alone, drove her further and further along.

Head down, hamstrings humming, she ploughed on.

And on.

And on.

'What wouldn't I give for a helicopter now!' she panted, bending double to catch her breath.

Her heart was on its last ventricles, pounding

so hard that the zip on her Puffa jacket was loosening.

'Hang on in there, Claudius,' she wheezed. 'I'm coming.'

Stride, groan, squelch, groan.

Stride, groan, squelch, groan.

Twelve trudges further, she toppled again.

Nelly lifted her elbow from the mire and wrenched her leg up with both hands. Her knee and calf lifted free from the ooze, to reveal nothing but a sock.

'Oh nooooooo!' she groaned, scrabbling hopelessly around in the ooze. But her wellington boot was lost.

Staggering to her feet, she hobbled on.

'I *will* get to the road! I *will* get to the road!' she wheezed.

Ten metres further on, over she went again.

With a spin and a twist, her walking stick javelined from her hand.

'The *English Adventurer*!' she gasped, as its handle disappeared below the ooze.

As the walking stick sank, Nelly's heart sank

with it. The puff in her lungs had thinned to a wisp. Did she have enough adventure still in her to make it?

'I'm Nelly the Monster Sitter! I'm Nelly the Monster Sitter!' she panted under her breath. 'I'm Nelly the Monster Sitter and I will get to the road!'

Stagger, stumble, squelch, gasp.

Stagger, stumble, squelch, gasp.

Nelly soldiered on.

'Nearly there! Nearly there! Nearly there!' she wheezed.

Minus one wellington and a top-notch walking stick, Nelly was at last approaching the road.

Wriggling her sodden sock free from a pocket of ooze, she forged on with her spirits recharged.

'Look out, Scab,' she panted, 'here I come!'

Finally, thankfully, wearily, miraculously, Nelly staggered to the roadside boundary of the marsh. Back arched, legs bent and shoulders heaving she gulped oxygen back into her lungs.

'I made it!' she panted.

With the stagger of a bog monster she dragged

herself to the embankment and fell in a heap on the grass.

'Keep going,' she panted, lifting herself to her feet and then running for all she was worth in the direction of the trees.

Her direct bee-line across the marsh had left her with a hundred-metre sprint to the fly-tipping point.

Hurtling on blindly, she cut left through a cat's cradle of loose barbed wire strands, and then on, on, on along the foot of the embankment.

Only as she approached the thicket of trees that surrounded the fly-tipping point did she allow herself to slow.

Falling to her knees, Nelly took time out to think.

She was only a few metres from the fly-tipping point now – close enough, she fancied, to hear the demonic panting of Jack Scab's dog.

More likely the panting was her own, but Nelly had no thoughts for herself. Right now, there was only one thing on her mind: a small furry prisoner in the pink paraffin can.

Ripping a fistful of grass from the field, she tossed it high in the air and watched it fall. It fell limply to the ground landing slightly forward of her knees. That was good news. What wind there was, was still heading west.

Nelly slipped her hand inside the pocket of her jeans and closed her fingers tightly around Hadrian's golden stool. She had left the Digdiggs' home with ten Roman coins and the beginnings of a plan. How the beginnings of her plan would end, she really had no idea.

16

Nelly crawled closer to the fly-tipping point. A slash of green Jeep was semi-visible through the tangle of sickly branches. Was that Scab's car?

A low muffled growl came from behind a pile of conifer branches. Was that Scab's dog?

She ducked down and swept her gaze round the thicket, but apart from a fractured jigsaw of black bin bags, sheet cardboard and discarded junk there was little she could see.

'I must be mad,' she murmured, using her fingernails to prise the ten golden coins carefully apart.

With another glance through the trees, she pulled the scrunchy from her hair and began putting the coins into every pocket she had. With just one coin remaining in her hand, she prepared to execute her plan.

'I *will* be mad!' she whispered, slowly and deliberately cupping one hand over the bump on her forehead and then bursting like a lunatic through the branches and into the clearing.

'HELLO!' she squawked. 'COULD YOU HELP ME PUT THIS COIN IN THE PARKING METER, PLEASE?'

Had Nelly caught sight of Jack Scab before she charged into the clearing, she might have been tempted to run the other way. For Scab was without doubt the scariest-looking human she had ever seen.

His face had the thin drawn features of a skeleton's skull, his skin the greasy pallor of wet papier mâché.

Mustering all her courage, she marched boldly across the garbage-strewn clearing to confront him.

'SATAN!' snapped Scab, pulling a bullwhip from the inside pocket of his grimy denim jacket and cracking it loudly.

Nelly held her nerve, together with the golden Roman coin. She was now a metre from

Scab's shotgun-pellet stare, and boy, did he look unhappy!

'SATAN!' he growled again.

Nelly fixed his stare with her own.

'Excuse me, excuse me, excuse me!' she squawked. 'Could you help me put this coin in the parking meter, please? It doesn't fit, it doesn't fit, it doesn't fit!'

'SATAN! HERE! NOW!' hissed Scab, throwing a poisonous glare across the clearing towards a scrap heap of car exhausts, cardboard and garbage.

A landslide of festering bin bags toppled from behind the carcass of a disused fridge and the white pigeon-egg eyes of the blind dog turned towards them.

Nelly tipped her head slightly for her first glimpse of Scab's hellhound.

'There it is!' she thought, oblivious to the Frankenstein features of the dog but overjoyed to see the pink of the paraffin can clamped between its jaws.

A second crack of the bullwhip and Satan sprang to Jack Scab's side.

Nelly kept her eyes fixed firmly on Scab but felt the hot breath of his dog steaming her legs as it sniffed blindly around the area of her shins and knees. Encouraged by the glimpse of the paraffin can, she raised the Roman coin with renewed purpose and thrust it boldly into the blistered palm of Jack Scab's hand.

'I CAN'T GET THIS COIN IN THE SLOT! CAN YOU GET IT IN THE SLOT?'

Scab's black pellet eyes glanced at the coin, and then shot through the thicket in all directions. He had just finished dumping a Jeep-load of illegal trash. This was company he hadn't expected and didn't want.

'What slot?' he drawled through brown, nicotine-stained teeth. He was beginning to lose patience with this gibbering idiot.

'THE PARKING METER SLOT!' squawked Nelly, removing her hand from her forehead to reveal the huge bump on her head.

Scab's eyes fixed themselves on the bump.

Who was this wild-haired lunatic with one boot on and one boot off and a bump on her

head the size of a field mushroom?

His brow furrowed and his lips thinned.

'What parking meter?' he drawled. 'There ain't no parkin' meters round here.'

Nelly turned and pointed across the clearing to a broken exhaust pipe stacked against a pile of rubble and hardcore.

'THAT PARKING METER!' she squawked. 'Can't you see it? I'm going to get a fine if I don't get my coin in the parking meter!'

Scab looked down at the coin that Nelly had forced into his hand.

With his attention distracted, Nelly seized the opportunity to snatch another glance at his dog. It was more hideous than she had at first thought. Its body and neck were solid muscle, tapering impossibly from powerful mastiff jaws to small and scrabbling Jack Russell legs. Its coat was a mass of cigarette burns and bullwhip weals. To her dismay, Satan was gnawing at the neck of the paraffin can, splintering the plastic like a bone.

Scab took a second glance at the coin.

'Hell's teeth!' he gasped, raising it to his eyes and then flipping it from head to tails between his fingers. 'Where did you get this from?'

Nelly played dumb, and stared blankly into Scab's piercing eyes.

'I don't want a parking fine, I don't want a parking fine!' she squawked.

Scab turned the coin over again, and then clamped his fingers tightly around it.

He was no archaeologist, but he knew a Roman coin when he saw one.

He knew a nutcase when he saw one too, and there was one standing directly in front of him now.

'Soooo,' he probed cautiously. 'You reckon that's a parking meter, do you?'

Nelly nodded. 'That's my parking meter,' said Nelly, pointing to the broken exhaust pipe, 'and that's my car.'

Scab followed the line of Nelly's outstretched finger. She was pointing to the old and rusting carcass of the fridge.

Scab closed his fingers tightly around the

golden coin and smiled the thinnest of thin-lipped smiles. An opportunity was forming in his villainous mind.

With a click of his fingers and a glare at his dog, he made his way across the clearing towards the fridge.

Nelly's eyes darted to the paraffin can. Was Claudius alive? Was he still inside the plastic can? As long as Satan had it clamped between his teeth, there was no way of knowing.

She glanced down at her soggy sock in time to see Satan tighten his jaws around the tooth-punctured can and scamper away across the clearing.

Scab stood beside the exhaust pipe with a drop-shouldered slouch, and waited for Nelly to join him.

How was she going to get Satan to release the can?

'Have you had a bang on the 'ead, young lady?' he drawled, peering more closely at Nelly's face.

'I can't remember,' said Nelly blankly.

'You 'AVE 'ad a bang on the 'ead, 'aven't you? That's a woppin' great bump you've got there.'

'I can't remember,' said Nelly.

'What's your name?' said Scab.

'I can't remember,' said Nelly.

'Where do you live?' said Scab.

'I can't remember,' said Nelly.

Nelly stared blankly ahead as Scab's eyes dropped from the bump on her forehead to the coin that was now nestling in his outstretched palm.

'Have you got any other coins like this that I could try in the meter?' he asked.

Nelly stared vacantly ahead of her and slipped her right hand inside her Puffa jacket pocket.

'Here's one,' she said, placing a second Roman coin in Scab's palm.

'Here's one,' she said, pulling another from her other pocket with her left hand.

'Here's one,' she said, prising a third from the back pocket of her jeans.

'Here's two,' she said, pulling a pair from the left front pocket of her jeans.

'Here's four,' she said, plucking a small fortune from the right.

Scab's lips puckered with delight as, one by

one, nine more golden coins spilled like a slot machine jackpot into his palm.

Nelly resisted a shudder as his hollow skeletal cheeks lifted into a toothless grin and his grimy twig of an arm snapped reassuringly around her shoulders.

'Let's see if I can feed the meter for you,' said Scab, leading Nelly gently past the fridge to the exhaust pipe.

Nelly threw another hopeful glance down at the paraffin can and walked zombie-legged beside him.

'Oh look!' said Jack Scab, hitting on a greed-fuelled plan to capitalize on Nelly's short-term insanity. 'Oh look, you're right,' he cooed, raising one of the Roman coins between his thumb and index finger and pretending to feed it into the exhaust pipe.

'You're right, young lady. These coins don't fit into this parking meter at all, do they? That's because these are the wrong sort of coins. These are foreign coins. These are worthless coins. No good for a parking meter at all.'

'But I don't want a fine, I don't want a fine!' squawked Nelly.

'Don't you worry about fines,' said Scab. 'I'll pay your parking fine for you. Now you just tell me how you bumped your head. And where you found these coins.'

'I can't remember,' said Nelly.

Scab's top lip curled with frustration. He had ten golden coins in his hand, but a treasure chest in his sights.

'You're very muddy,' he probed. 'Did you find them on the marsh?'

'Definitely not,' Nelly mumbled.

'At least we're getting somewhere,' smiled Scab. 'Now think very hard. Where exactly did you find these worthless coins?'

Nelly glanced at the paraffin can and thought very hard. She thought harder than she had ever thought in her life, and then smiled inwardly. The key part of her plan had suddenly come to her.

'Have you seen my pig?' she squawked.

'WHAT?' said Scab.

226

'I've lost my pet pig. Have you seen it?' asked Nelly blankly.

Scab's smile fell from his face. What on earth was she wittering on about now?

'Never mind your pig,' he snapped, 'try and remember where you found these worthless coins.'

Nelly's face darkened and her bottom lip began to tremble. With the scream of a banshee, she raised her only wellington and stamped hard on the ground.

'I WANT MY PIG! I WANT MY PIG!' she screamed, producing a tantrum that even Asti would have been proud of.

Jack Scab ran his hands frantically through his grease-caked hair and Satan sprang up on all fours. First parking meters and now pigs? This girl was a total fruit loop!

'I WANT MY PIG!' squealed Nelly again, spinning round in circles and waving her arms in the air.

'OK, OK!' screamed Jack Scab. 'I'll find your pig AFTER you've remembered where you found these COINS!'

'NOWWWW!!!!' stamped Nelly. 'FIND MY PIGGY NOWWWWW!!!'

'What does your pig look like?' sighed Scab.

'It's pink,' said Nelly. 'And about this big,' she said, holding out her hands and widening them to the size of a paraffin can.

'There's your pig!' said Scab, dropping to the floor and clamping both hands around the paraffin can that Satan had clenched between his teeth.

'THERE'S MY PIG!' agreed Nelly.

'DROP, SATAN!' hissed Scab, trying to wrench the paraffin can free from the dog's jaws. 'DROP, I SAID!'

Satan was having none of it. He had good reason to believe there was a meal inside that paraffin can and he wasn't about to let it go. Nelly winced as the neck of the buckled can began to crumple under the vice-like pressure of his jaws. Her eyes widened as Scab hauled the can upwards with Satan attached, lifting his dog from the ground.

'DROP!' hissed Scab. 'Drop the damned

pig!' he screeched, kneeing the dog in its emaciated ribs.

Satan released the can for a split second and then clamped hold of it again. The higher Scab lifted, the tighter Satan gripped. The tighter Satan gripped, the more the paraffin can buckled.

Nelly began to wonder whether the end of her plan would signal the end of Claudius too. Alive or dead, much more of this and he would be crushed like a banger in a car crusher.

Jack Scab released his hold on the can and took his bullwhip from his jacket pocket. Moving three steps backwards he drew it over his shoulder and sent a stinging whip crack bee-lining for Satan's nose.

The tip of the whip connected like a hornet, sending Satan yelping in one direction and the paraffin can bouncing in another.

Nelly darted after the paraffin can and scooped it up.

'PIGGYWIG!' she cooed, cradling the imaginary pet to her bosom. 'Are you all right?

Did that nasty doggy hurt you?'

'I'm fine,' whispered the voice of Claudius from deep inside the can. 'Did Nero make it safely home?'

Nelly's heart leaped. Claudius was safe!

'Don't worry, piggywig,' she smiled. 'Everything's fine now.'

'Stop calling me piggywig,' whispered Claudius. 'I might be strong and I might be tough and I might be fast and I might be secretive. I might be a little bit bigger around the midriff, but I'm no piggywig!'

Nelly wiped the smile from her face and looked blankly into Jack Scab's eyes. Now it was time for some real fun.

'OK,' hissed Jack Scab, who was fast running out of patience. 'You've got your piggy porkin' plastic pet back, NOW THINK. Where did you find these coins?'

Nelly stroked the bump on her head gently and then smiled. 'I REMEMBER!' she squawked.

Scab wrapped the whip excitedly round its handle and stuffed it back in his pocket.

'That's good,' he hissed. 'Now remember EXACTLY where were you when you found them?'

Nelly cuddled the paraffin can and fixed Scab with fluttering eyes.

'Do you know the marsh?' she said.

'Yes!' said Scab excitedly.

'It wasn't the marsh,' said Nelly.

'You said that earlier!' snapped Scab. 'We've already established it wasn't the marsh. Now where was it?'

'Do you know the fields that have been ploughed?' said Nelly mischievously.

'The Crabtree Farm fields? YES!' squeaked Scab, almost beside himself with excitement. 'They were ploughed in October!'

'It wasn't there either,' said Nelly.

Scab's face twitched with anxiety.

'Do you know the woods?' asked Nelly.

'The Crabtree woods?' said Scab, almost wetting himself with the tension.

'I found the chest in the Crabtree woods,' said Nelly. 'Yes, it's all coming back to me now,' she swooned.

'Chest? Chest, you say?' drooled Scab.

'I was digging in the woods for worms to go fishing with.'

'Yes, yes,' snapped Scab. 'Never mind the fishing – get back to the woods!'

'I was digging with my spade when I found a buried chest. It was full to the brim with those coins.'

'Coins? Coins?' Scab drooled. 'How many coins?'

'Thousands. Millions maybe,' said Nelly. 'I was trying to count them when the lid fell down and hit me on the head.'

'Never mind lids and heads,' gasped Scab, 'where EXACTLY can I find that chest?'

A cloud passed over Nelly's eyes.

'I remember what the grass looked like,' she murmured.

'Yes,' said Scab, racing to his car and pulling a pencil and notebook from the glove compartment.

'It was green,' said Nelly, stroking her chin vaguely. 'The grass was definitely green.'

Scab lifted his pencil and slumped.

'Wait! I remember now,' said Nelly, determined to send Scab and his hellhound on the biggest wild goose chase of their lives.

'The grass was far far far away from the marsh on the far side of the woods,' said Nelly. 'Near a tree,' she added.

'Which tree?' squeaked Scab, scribbling furiously. 'What kind of tree was it? There are thousands of trees in the woods.'

Nelly stroked her bump thoughtfully and closed her eyes. 'I can see branches,' she said. 'And a trunk . . . with roots at the bottom. Yes, it was definitely a tree that had branches, and a trunk and some roots!'

Scab's face twitched again.

'Oak tree? Ash tree? Sycamore? Holly? Lime? Cedar? Maple?'

'It was a big tree,' said Nelly as unhelpfully as she could. 'Well, big to medium . . . to small.'

Scab screwed his notebook into a ball and hurled it at a pile of rotting garbage bags.

'You'll have to come with us,' he said, booting

Satan up the backside and ushering him into back of his Jeep.

'I'm not allowed to go with strangers,' said Nelly. 'I can draw you a map.'

Scab's eyes lit up, and then narrowed as he realised the notebook that Nelly would need to draw on had been hurled into the bushes.

'Satan, fetch the notebook' he snapped, despatching his dog into the garbage bags, with a crack of his whip.

Satan sprang from the Jeep, retrieved the screwed up notebook and dropped it at Nelly's feet.

Nelly plucked the pencil from the spine of the book and set about drawing a plate of spaghetti with some meatballs and ball of string entwined.

'There you go,' she said, placing the treasure map into Scab's bony palm.

Scab took one look at it and kicked his tyre in a fit of frustration.

'Satan up!' he growled, hurling the notebook over his shoulder, and ordering his dog back into the Jeep.

'Do you have a mobile phone?' asked Nelly. 'If you give me your number I could ring you if I remember any more. I mean once my bump's gone down I might be able to remember everything!'

With his notebook consigned to the bushes, and nothing else to write on, Scab ripped the tax disc from his windscreen and scribbled his contact numbers on the reverse side.

'YOU BE SURE TO RING ME IF YOU DO REMEMBER ANYTHING,' he snarled, screeching out of the clearing with a scream of brakes, and rocketing up Bitter Avenue in the direction of the Crabtree woods.

'I won't,' smiled Nelly, breathing a momentous sigh of relief.

Nelly stood alone in the clearing and watched the cloud of exhaust fumes sprinkle like pepper on to the floor.

'You can come out now, Claudius,' she sighed.

17

'Genius!' said Claudius, squeezing his moustache through the neck of the paraffin can and then easing himself out like a furry cork.

'They'll be in the woods for hours!' he laughed.

'They'll be there for weeks if I have my way,' smiled Nelly, punching Scab's home and mobile telephone numbers into her mobile phone.

'Well, they'll be gone long enough for me to make it home safely,' said Claudius. 'Lawdy, that dog's breath smelled!'

Nelly looked at her watch. It was five past six. Her dad would be waiting for her by the road bridge.

She looked at her soggy sock, she looked at her mud-caked coat, she looked at her single wellington boot.

Her mum and dad were going to kill her.

'If you don't mind, Claudius, I won't accompany you home,' she sighed. 'I'm late enough as it is, and you'll get home to your family much quicker without me.'

'But how . . . ?'

'Taxi,' smiled Nelly, raising her mobile and punching out the short code for her dad.

Claudius hopped on to the toe of her wellington, and waited to say his goodbyes.

'Hi, Dad,' she said. 'Sorry, there's been a change of plan. Can you pick me up from the Bitter Avenue layby? I'll explain later,' she said with a nibble of her lip.

'It's going to take some explaining,' smiled Claudius, rubbing his chest with his paws to wipe his fur clean of chilli sauce.

'Go now, while the wind is in the right direction,' said Nelly, 'and don't stop off at any kebab shops along the way!'

'I won't!' shuddered Claudius.

'Look out for my wellington and my walking stick too!' laughed Nelly.

'Will do!' chuckled Claudius.

'And send my love to Nero and the kids!' added Nelly. 'All one hundred and twenty-one of them.' She beamed with a pat of her belly.

With a wave of his paw and a twitch of his mustard moustache, Claudius vanished into the undergrowth.

Nelly hopped, in an ungainly way, to the layby and sat down on the roadside verge.

'Mum is going to absolutely murder me,' she groaned, wringing out the toe of her sock.

18

When Claudius returned home he was greeted with the shrieks of unbridled delight.

When Nelly returned home, she was greeted with gasps of unbridled horror.

'What have you been doing?' squeaked her mum as she stepped shamefaced from the car. 'Look at the state of you! I thought you were going monster sitting, not mud-wrestling!'

Nelly dumped her one remaining wellington on the front step and raced up the stairs to the bathroom.

'And she's lost my walking stick!' grouched her dad, limping into the hallway.

'I'll buy you another one!' shouted Nelly, with a slam of the bathroom door.

'You'll buy me a new washing machine if all that mud clogs it up!' growled her mum.

* * *

That evening, a sparklingly clean Nelly stood alone on the patio with a bump on her forehead and a fistful of Snowball's barley straw in her hand. Tossing the straw high in the air, she watched with keen-eyed interest as it fluttered to the patio to the left of her feet. Just as she suspected, the wind was changing direction to a south-westerly.

'No probs,' she smiled, pulling her phone from her pocket and tapping out Scab's number.

'Jack, it's me,' she said. 'I've just remembered. You're in the wrong woods. I meant the woods on the other side of town next to the Badley Hall Estate. Sorry to mess you about. Good luck.'

Over the next two months Scab's search for the rest of the Roman treasure hoard would take him to every tree in Lowbridge, then further west to the sewage plant and finally to the north-west, where he would be arrested for digging holes on the golf course. Oh, and car tax evasion too.

The moment he was released from bail, Nelly handed his home phone number to the police.

His address was traced, and his wicked trade in patchwork quilts was ended.

As for Satan? Well, Satan was taken to an animal rescue centre.

As yet, not surprisingly, there have been no takers.

1

It was Christmas Day in the afternoon, and the Morton household was groaning. Nelly's mum had had too much nut roast, Nelly's dad had had too many Czechoslovakian lagers, Nelly had had too many sticky dates and Asti hadn't had enough presents.

'What a totally rubbish Christmas,' she fumed. 'I hardly got anything to unwrap, and the presents I DID get were total poop. I mean, what on earth does Auntie Vi think I'm going to do with a *Rainbow Pixie* colouring book? I'm twelve!'

Nelly's mum waited for a piece of nut roast to unlodge itself from the lining of her stomach wall and then reached for the chocolate Brazils.

'Asti, don't be so ungrateful. The reason you got fewer presents to unwrap this year is because you asked for money. And as for Auntie Vi, you

know full well her brain went years ago. It's a
wonder she remembered it was Christmas at all.'

'It's the thought that counts,' said Nelly,
thumbing creatively through the pages of the
Thomas the Tank Engine Bumper Activity Book her
loopy aunt had sent to her.

Asti tore her cracker hat from her head and screwed it into a ball.

'Well, if it's the thought that counts, I'd have THOUGHT that Auntie Vi could have had a brain operation in time for Christmas, so that she wouldn't end up buying two-year-old presents for her twelve-year-old nieces. Plus, my sweet little sister, I'd have THOUGHT you might have remembered that my new favourite clothes colour is CERISE, which, in case you didn't know, is a deep cherry red colour and NOT a scummy splurge of green, yellow and turquoise swirls!'

Nelly lifted the tip of a purple felt tip from Edward the Engine's teeth and turned to her sister. 'What's wrong with green, yellow and turquoise swirls?' she enquired innocently.

'Nothing,' said Asti, 'unless it's on the T-shirt your one and only twin sister bought you for Christmas. Then it looks like a bucket of sick!'

'Freeb loved hers,' smirked Nelly.

But Asti wasn't listening.

'And if it's the thought that counts,' she hissed, determined to press her point further, 'if it's the thought that counts, I'd have THOUGHT someone in my family could have thought about buying me some surprise expensive presents, like proper make-up, or some surprise expensive trainers, or at least an iPod, just so I would have SOME surprise decent presents to open on Christmas morning NOT JUST MONEY!'

'You asked for money, you got money,' said her mum.

'Yes, well I didn't mean ONLY money,' protested Asti. 'I meant surprise presents as well!'

'Not getting any surprise presents *was* a kind of surprise,' smirked Nelly.

'Shut up, Freak-over,' said Asti.

'Charades anyone?' suggested Nelly's dad from his favourite armchair in front of the telly.

'No thanks,' came the unanimous response.

'Asti, you did have some surprise presents to open,' said her mum, nibbling the shell off a sugared almond. 'You had some trainer socks, three CDs and a Lather of London Home Bath and Spa experience.'

'And you had a mini calculator to help you with your maths,' said Nelly.

'Exactly!' said Asti. 'How rubbish is that!' she hissed, launching her *Rainbow Pixie* book across the lounge and folding her arms with a scowl.

Nelly's mum shrugged her shoulders and waved her index finger indecisively across a newly opened box of liquorice allsorts.

'I don't know, what IS wrong with the kids of today?' she sighed. 'Why, when we were children every present was a treat, no matter how big or small or inexpensive, wasn't it, Clifford?'

Nelly's dad nodded absent-mindedly.

'Clifford!' yelled Nelly's mum. 'Will you stop gawping at the telly and engage your family in some meaningful conversation. Just because no one will play charades with you, you don't have to turn into a Christmas couch potato. Christmas Day is a special day, a day for families to unite in merriment and festive joy.'

Nelly's dad lifted his left hand from the arm of the chair. He had decided to unite in merriment with another can of lager instead.

Nelly's mum sighed and went back to the liquorice allsorts.

Nelly grabbed a fistful of felt tips and set about giving Edward the Engine a new Technicolor moustache.

Asti fumed. Asti festered. And then Asti flipped.

'What do you mean, Freeb liked hers? Freeb loved her *what* exactly?'

Nelly's mum paused in mid-crunch. Her dad lowered his lager from his lips and Nelly lifted the purple felt tip uncertainly from the page. No one in the room was exactly sure what Asti was talking about now, or who exactly she was talking to. The cluc came when she picked up her screwed-up party hat, scrunched it into an even tighter ball and then launched it in the direction of Nelly's head.

'What did you say?' asked Nelly, pretending not to notice as the missile bounced off her shoulder.

Asti leaned forward on the sofa, unfolded her arms and placed her hands on her knees.

'I said,' she growled, 'what did you mean

earlier when you said, "Freeb loved hers"?'

Nelly calmly put the finishing touches to Edward the Engine's techno moustache, placed the felt tip tidily back in its slot and smiled.

'I meant, Asti dearest, that Freeb really liked the T-shirt I bought her for Christmas. It was the same design as the one I bought you, only with one more armhole and four sizes bigger.'

Asti gasped, shuddered uncontrollably and turned to instant icicles. Her lips thinned, her eyeballs froze, her face frosted.

And then she cracked.

'YOU ACTUALLY MEAN TO SAY YOU BOUGHT *ME* THE SAME CHRISTMAS PRESENT AS ONE OF YOUR DISGUSTING HAIRY-FACED MONSTER FRIENDS!' she screeched, leaping from the sofa.

'*ME!* YOUR OWN SISTER! The same Christmas present as a monster!'

Nelly smiled to herself. It was always good to see Asti in a fizz.

'As I said before, Astilbe,' Nelly chuckled, 'it's the thought that counts. And anyway, Freeb didn't think her T-shirt looked like sick, she thought it looked beeeeeeautiful!'

'THAT'S BECAUSE FREEB IS SICK TOO! SHE'S SICK ON LEGS!' screeched Asti. 'IN FACT SHE'S A SICK LITTLE FLEA-RIDDEN GORILLA CROSSED WITH A SICK LITTLE ONION-EYED DANGLY RED RUG!'

'The correct term is Huffaluk,' said Nelly, plucking another felt tip from the box. 'If you must know, the Dendrileg twins loved their swirly hotchpotch T-shirts as well.'

That was the final straw for Asti. It was Christmas Day. She'd had no surprise presents, no cerise clothing, a mini calculator, and now her sister had lumped her Christmas present in with a bunch of dribbling monsters.

'It's the thought that counts,' smiled Nelly for the third time, deliberately trying to whip Asti up from a fizz to a froth.

A froth it was.

'The thought that counts?' she screeched, hysterically. 'It isn't thoughts that count at Christmas, it's PRESENTS! It's PRESENTS AND

MONEY! ANYONE KNOWS THAT! You can't wrap thoughts up in wrapping paper and sellotape, can you? You can't tie a ribbon round a thought!' *Dear Santa, I'll have a stocking full of thoughts, please. No, make that a sack full of thoughts. All I want for Christmas is my two front thoughts.* I don't think so. EVERYONE WANTS THOUGHTS FOR CHRISTMAS, DO THEY? WELL, HERE'S SOME THOUGHTS. Thought One: This Christmas sucks and so do all the presents I got. Thought Two: Aunts and uncles and grandmas who can't buy decent presents for their nieces or granddaughters should be sent to prison or made to have a brain transplant. Thought Three: Sisters called Nelly who buy sisters called Asti the same presents as monsters should be sellotaped to a tree in the snow for ten days and made to freeze to within a centimetre of their life.'

'What if there's no snow?' enquired Nelly innocently.

Asti ignored her.

'Thought Four,' she said, starting to run out of thoughts. 'Er . . .' she stammered.

'Christmas stinks!' she growled. 'Christmas trees stink, Christmas puddings stink, Christmas cake stinks, Christmas carols stink, in fact everything beginning with Christmas STINKS! What does my lovely family think of those thoughts then?'

There was an uncomfortable pause. Mostly due to shock, partly due to indigestion.

Nelly feared the worst as her mum looked darkly at her husband and then bit the head off a jelly baby.

'The only thing that stinks around here, young lady, is your attitude. I've never heard such an ungrateful outburst. Especially on Christmas Day! Go to your room!'

The tip of Nelly's felt tip buckled. It was years since either of them had been told to go to their room. Was it legal to send a twelve-year-old to a room? She decided it must be. Especially if the twelve-year-old in question had the mental age of a walnut.

'Don't worry, I'm going anyway,' said Asti, flouncing out of the lounge in the direction of the stairs. 'I'm going to my room right now to count how much money I got for Christmas, and do you know the first thing I'm going to buy with it?'

No one remaining in the lounge felt inclined to ask.

'A box of matches and a gallon of petrol!' shouted Asti. 'And don't ask what I'm going to do with them!'

Even by Asti's standards it was a fit and a half.

'And here's another thought!' she screeched, from the top of the stairs. 'I'm not helping with the washing up. HA!'

Asti's bedroom door shut with a slam. And then reopened.

'UNLESS YOU PAY ME!'

Slam!

2

It's an unfortunate fact of Christmas Day that after all the fun and the games and the merriment, after all the present opening and turkey carving and cracker pulling, the fizzy drink swigging, sweetie munching and *I'm a Celebrity Loo Brush Get Me Out of Here* Christmas Special TV watching, at some point, sadly and inevitably, a tea towel must loom. Several tea towels, in fact, and at Nelly's house, owing to her mum's inability to cook anything without welding it to the pan, a lorryload of industrial strength kitchen scourers.

Nelly stood beside her mum and dad in the kitchen and stared glumly at an Everest of washing up.

'How about I do my nut roast pan and you do the rest?' suggested Mum.

'How about you do your nut roast pan and Asti does the rest?' suggested Nelly.

Nelly's mum and dad frowned. Asti was in disgrace big time, and even washing up a mountain of dirty dishes wouldn't bail her from her bedroom cell.

'Heads you wash, tails you wash,' said Nelly's dad, flipping the silver sixpence he had found in his Christmas pudding,

Nelly sighed, opened the cupboard under the sink and retrieved the rubber gloves. 'I bet the Queen never has to do any washing up,' she said with a rubbery squeak.

'You're probably right,' said Nelly's mum, assisting Nelly with the second glove. 'It would be lovely if we could just click our fingers and the washing up was done. But then royal servants are in short supply on the Montelimar Estate.'

Nelly raised the pair of yellow rubber gloves like a surgeon, put the plug in the empty sink, did the business with the washing-up liquid, and plunged the first fistful of dirty cutlery into the soapy water.

'I bet Furry Liquid would do the job in half the time,' she said. 'The Squurms at Number 322 do their washing up with Furry Liquid.'

Nelly's dad swooped on the first knives and forks to emerge from the suds and began rubbing them vigorously with a tea towel.

'I wonder what monsters do for Christmas,' said Nelly's mum. 'I wonder what they eat for Christmas dinner. I wonder if they celebrate Christmas at all?'

'They do,' said Nelly, deciding to let the Yorkshire pudding tray soak for a little bit longer. 'At least Dendrilegs do.'

'How do you know that?' asked her dad, pretending to tie his shoelaces in an attempt to avoid the Yorkshire pudding tray.

'Lump told me,' said Nelly. 'In fact Lump and Poltis invited me to their house for a Christmas celebration today.'

Nelly's dad lifted a dinner plate from the drainer and then put it back down. 'Invited you to their house, Nelly? On Christmas Day? Then why didn't you go? Why didn't you say?'

Nelly ground a kitchen scourer into a particularly stubborn piece of burnt parsnip and then turned to her mum and dad in surprise.

'I thought you'd want me to be at home with you on Christmas Day! Hey, I DO want to be at home with you on Christmas Day! Christmas Day is a special day. A day for families to unite in merriment and festive joy. That's what you said earlier.'

Nelly's mum and dad raised their eyes in the direction of Asti's bedroom.

'Merriment and festive joy seem to be in short supply in our house this Christmas,' said her mum, stopping her tea towel in mid wipe.

Nelly's dad nodded. 'If I were you, Nelly, I'd much rather be monstering it up with my friends.'

Nelly looked down into the washing-up bowl and then sideways at the mountain of crockery and crusty Teflon still waiting to be scoured. Suddenly the awful task ahead of her had a clear and worthwhile purpose! Clear this lot, wipe down the draining board and bingo! She could be on her way to the Dendrilegs' for her first ever Christmas Day at a monster's house!

'Are you sure you don't mind?' she asked excitedly, plunging three dinner plates into the suds at once. 'I'll quite happily stay at home with you if you prefer. I'll even play Charades with you if you really want me to.'

Nelly's mum's eyebrows wilted at the thought.

'No one wants to play Charades, thank you, Nelly,' she said firmly. 'Christmas Day at the Dendrilegs' sounds much more fun. In fact your dad and I would come with you as well if we were invited, wouldn't we, Clifford? And if it didn't mean leaving Asti on her own in the house. The mood she's in, she'll probably torch the place.'

'Yes, Nelly, you go. We can play games tomorrow,' said Nelly's dad, reluctant to give up on the idea of Charades altogether. 'You go and have some Christmas fun with the Dendrilegs. If the invitation is still open, that is. I can't give you a lift in the car though,' he added hastily. 'I've had too many lagers.'

'And I've had too many wine gums,' said Nelly's mum, equally anxious to avoid Christmas Day taxi duties.

'That's OK,' said Nelly, 'they only live up the road. I can walk there in five minutes! No taxi drivers required this evening!'

'Excellent!' said Nelly's dad, smiling at the prospect of more Czechoslovakian lagers.

'You'd better ring your monster friends first though,' said her mum. 'They might have made other arrangements.'

'I doubt it,' smiled Nelly, 'but I promise I'll ring just the same.'

3

With the mountain of washing up finally conquered and seven soggy tea towels hung neatly out to dry, Nelly raced out of the kitchen and up to her bedroom. Actually she diverted slightly to listen at Asti's door, but their was little to glean from the sound of Asti counting and recounting her money. Except that, for a short while at least, Asti was loaded. With a shrug of indifference, Nelly padded into her own bedroom, sat excitedly on her bed and reached for her monster sitting phone.

Her call to the Dendrilegs was greeted by a crescendo of suckery thwucks and the sound of tentacles slapping against tentacles.

'That's wonderful news, Nelly!' thwucked Lump, getting into an excitable tangle with his phone cord as he switched the phone between four ears. 'Just wait till I tell Poltis and the children! Of course you can come round for Christmas tea! We'd be delighted to see you! We've got lots of num nums and there'll be a wonderful surprise for you later! – When will you be here? Bog and Blotch loved their T-shirts, by the way, in fact they've been wearing them all day. It really was very kind of you to buy them a present. We've got a big surprise for you too, Nelly! I hope you like it.'

'I'll be with you at seven o'clock,' said Nelly, just about managing to squeeze seven words in edgeways.

'Pleeeease no later than nine, Nelly,' thwucked Lump. 'Someone very special will be coming to our house at nine! You wouldn't want to miss it for the world! Please promise me you'll be here by nine o'clock at the very latest!'

Nelly flopped back on to her bed and smiled. She was a little intrigued now. 'I won't miss it,' she said, 'and I promise you I'll be with you by one second past seven at the latest! But please don't go to a lot of fuss on my account. I've already had a big Christmas dinner, so the last thing I need is lots of monster nosh to eat. Mind you, I can always find room for a num num! Are they Pirrin and Ug flavour?'

'They are!' squawked Lump with a suckery thwuck. 'Have you had them before?'

'At the Cowcumbers'!' laughed Nelly. 'They're scrummy!'

'We'll save you the longest one,' thwucked Lump. 'Do you like churly freeps too?' thwucked Lump. 'Do you like Nibnobs? What flavour Nibnobs do you like?'

'STOP!' laughed Nelly. 'All this talk of food is making me giddy! Yes, I like churly freeps and no, I've never tried Nibnobs but I'm sure I'll like them too! Now stop talking, Lump, and start letting me get ready,' she chuckled. 'I'll see you at seven o'clock! Goodbye!'

'Do you like—'

'Goodbye!' said Nelly, slamming the receiver back into place and cutting Lump off in mid-thwuck.

'What IS he like?' she smiled. 'And what SHALL I wear?'

4

It was a smarter than usual Nelly who skipped down the stairs into the hallway that evening. Same red trainers, but a new pair of indigo blue jeans that she'd been given for Christmas, and a cream blouse that she always saved for special occasions. After all, a trip to a monster's house on Christmas Day wasn't just special, it was off the scale!

'I'll be back by ten!' she shouted, slapping a brand new Christmas Post-it on the mirror in the hallway and grabbing her Puffa jacket from the coat stand. 'Number 93 Sweet Street!' she shouted, reading the Dendrilegs' address out loud enough for her mum and dad to hear.

'Have fun!' shouted her dad, uniting in merriment with his sixth Czechoslovakian lager of the day.

'Say Happy Christmas to the Bendywotsits!' shouted her mum, leafing carefully through the envelopes in a box of After Eight mints.

'Dendrilegs, not Bendywotsits!' laughed Nelly.

'Hope they bite your head off!' shouted Asti from the top of the stairs. 'And suck all your blood out!'

'Happy Christmas to you too,' shouted Nelly, zipping up her Puffa jacket and opening the front door.

'No snow as usual,' she sighed, closing the front door behind her and stepping out into a frosty December night. She looked ruefully down at the snowless garden path, then threw a glance to the end of the path where the laurel hedge was glowing a warm orange colour beneath the street light.

'It never snows at Christmas,' she sighed, looking up at the rooftops of the houses opposite and imagining them for one moment iced deep and crisp and even.

She imagined a little more: the whole of Sweet Street transformed into a Christmas card, with robins perched on every gatepost, snowmen grinning coal black smiles from every garden, reindeers parked outside instead of cars, and snowflakes swirling like fresh Parmesan on to pavements fast disappearing under drifts.

Then she got real again. 'No snow as per rotten usual!' she sighed.

She zipped up her jacket to keep the bite of the air from her chest and peered dejectedly upwards at the starry December sky.

'No snow tomorrow either.'

With a clunk of the gate latch, Nelly turned right and set off in the direction of Number 93.

She looked at her watch. It was six minutes to seven. The Dendrilegs only lived thirteen doors away on the same side of the road, and if she wasn't careful she was in danger of arriving early.

Nelly didn't like to arrive early or late when she went visiting. On time was the only time for Nelly.

She looked at her watch again and deliberately slowed to a dawdle.

As she passed each of her neighbours' houses, she turned her head towards the darkly drawn

curtains and tried to imagine the festivities going on behind them. Lots of telly watching probably, some after-dinner dozing possibly. Each curtain she passed gave nothing away, remaining twitch-free and eerily still.

'Still' was a word that Nelly had always associated with Christmas Day. It was hard to explain, but somehow on Christmas Day, the air outdoors just seemed stiller than usual. Emptier. As though all the outside energy you would normally find in a street had somehow transferred inside, where it was needed for all the present opening, and carol singing, and cracker pulling and party gaming. Not outside where it was not.

This evening was no exception. Outside in Christmas Day Sweet Street anything and everything had been put on hold. There wasn't a soul to be seen or a car headlamp to be dipped. Everything was Christmas Day still. Everything was Christmas Day quiet.

Nelly continued on her way, trying to glance through a slender crack of light peeping out between the curtains of Number 97. She'd never met her neighbours at Number 97. Maybe they were monsters too. Nine-headed monsters, perhaps, with squirrel tails and webbed feet. Maybe there was a whole family of them, wearing nine party hats each, sitting around the dining room table eating a huge joint of Mungus with cranberry sauce and all the trimmings, whatever monster trimmings are. Who knows, maybe she would get a call from Number 97 one day too.

After ten more dawdling steps, Nelly checked her watch again. It was two minutes to seven and the Dendrilegs' front door was in sight. To kill a little more time before entering their gate, she stooped to retie her laces and adjusted the tinsel in her scrunchy.

OK. Seven o'clock on the dot. Nelly took a deep, excited breath and lifted the rubber door knocker of the Dendrilegs' yellow front door. It fell with an almost noiseless thud against the latex weatherproof coating.

If she hadn't knocked on the Dendrilegs' front door many times before, she might have lifted the knocker and rapped harder again. But Nelly knew better. She was very well acquainted with the rubbery thud of the door knocker at Number 93 and she knew what to expect.

On previous occasions when she had stood too close to the door, she had found herself totally spaghettied.

As a precaution, she took two large steps backwards and waited.

Before you could say 'Father Chris—' the front door of Number 93 flew open and a flurry of purple tentacles burst through the opening to greet her.

Nelly's eyes crossed comically as the tips of the Dendrilegs' arms waved and probed just millimetres from the end of her nose. 'Happy Christmas, Nelly!' thwucked Poltis, the Dendrileg mum.

'Yes, happy Christmas!' squeaked lots more tentacles at knee level.

Her smiling eyes greeted Poltis's four sparkling adult eyeballs and then dropped lower to acknowledge the eight more belonging to the Dendrileg twins, Bog and Blotch.

'Happy Christmas, Poltis!' Nelly laughed. 'Happy Christmas, twins! Where's your dad?'

'Lump is in the lounge, making a phone call,' thwucked Poltis. 'Why don't you come through and say hello?'

Nelly smiled but then took a half-step back again as the tentacles surged forward to embrace her.

'C'mon, Nelly,' thwucked Poltis. 'Give us a Christmas cuddle!'

'Yes, don't be shy,' suckery-thwucked Blotch.

Nelly took a quarter-step backwards and then decided she would have to give in. After all, it probably wouldn't be a traditional Dendrilegs Christmas without a traditional Dendrilegs cuddle.

'I'm all yours!' she giggled, closing her eyes and stepping forward bravely.

The instant they had hold of her, all three

Dendrilegs erupted into a chorus of squeaks and festive suckery thwucks. Nelly disappeared instantly amid a frenzy of friendly tentacles.

'Christmas at the Dendrilegs' is going to be fun!' she chuckled to herself as the yellow front door of Number 93 closed behind her.

5

'Stop tickling!' squeaked Nelly, trying to hand Poltis her coat as squiggle upon squiggle of purple tentacles shepherded her along the softly lit hallway and into the Dendrilegs' lounge.

'That's enough, children!' thwucked Lump, replacing the phone in its green and pink vinyl stand and approaching Nelly with a broad and goofy-toothed smile. 'Let our Christmas guest get her breath back!'

Bog and Blotch withdrew three of their purple tentacles obediently but then slipped a fourth into Nelly's hands.

'Come and sit next to us, Nelly,' said Bog. 'Come and sit on the sofa with us.'

Nelly handed Lump her Puffa jacket, closed her fingers fondly around the cold rubbery tips of the identical twins' arms and allowed them to lead her to the sofa.

'Sit in the middle,' thwucked Blotch, keen to claim an equal share of Nelly's attention. 'Sit in the middle, then that will be fair.'

Nelly stopped in mid-carpet.

'I think you should both give me a twirl first,' she beamed. 'Show me how nice you look in the new T-shirts I bought you.'

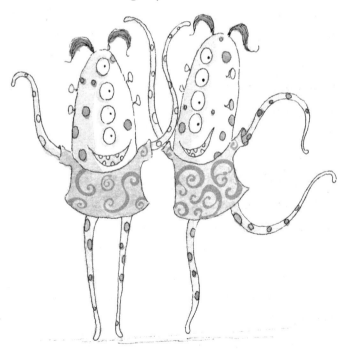

The eight emerald eyes of the twins looked down and sparkled like Christmas baubles.

Nelly smiled as the two Dendrileg children raised their tentacles and then spun like fairground rides across the carpet and back.

'We love them!' they thwucked. 'The colours are the best, and they fit us really well!'

'Pleased to hear it!' Nelly smiled, raising her hand to stop the twins from making themselves dizzy.

'We've got a surprise for you too later!' thwucked Blotch.

'Lots of surprises!' thwucked Bog.

'SSSSSHHHHH!' thwucked Lump. 'Not a word more.'

Blotch and Bog stared at the ceiling as if nothing had been said and then clapped their tentacles excitedly as their mum returned from the kitchen with a huge bowl of num nums.

'Now then, Nelly, tell us all about the Christmas you've been having!' thwucked Lump. 'I'm sure it's more exciting than ours.'

Nelly lifted a num num from the spaghetti-length tub and shook her head.

'No, it's been a bit boring this year,' she sighed. 'Until now, that is!' she crunched. 'Asti's been a real grump as usual, and it hasn't snowed again, as per usual. We never have a white Christmas EVER!'

'Yes, we remember you saying when you monster sat for us in the autumn. I'm sure it will snow soon. Then you can throw those snowballs at Asti you were telling us about.'

'No, it won't. It never snows,' sighed Nelly. 'At least not if I'm around. I could go to the North Pole and it probably wouldn't snow.'

'More num nums!' thwucked Poltis, thrusting the tub centimetres from the end of Nelly's nose. 'Try two at once! It's Christmas!'

Thoughts of snow melted away as the unmistakable strawberry aroma of Pirrin and Ug wafted deliciously from the bowl. Nelly removed another metre-long crunchy spiral and added it to the one she had already nibbled.

'Who needs snow when you've got num nums?' she crunched. 'Now then, why don't we all sit down?'

Bog and Blotch quickly lassoed an arm each and chaperoned Nelly excitedly towards the glistening white cushions that mushroomed the full length of the Dendrilegs' white and green PVC sofa.

'Remember you're in the middle, Nelly,' they thwucked, 'then it will be fair!'

Nelly lifted her num nums up out of harm's way, and dropped on to the middle cushion between the twins. Within seconds two friendly tentacles had slid on to her knee from each side of the sofa. She settled back into the cushions and looked round the room.

It was a long lounge – two rooms knocked through to make one, in fact. Directly ahead of her, at the far end of the room, there was a chimney breast clad in pink plastic bricks. Behind her, at the opposite end of the room, double doors leading to the garden were draped with lime green shower type curtains.

'I see you decorate your lounge at Christmas as well,' Nelly said, sweeping her gaze along a festive chain of giant green globules that were hanging from the ceiling like ogre's bogies.

'Dongles, yes!' thwucked Lump. 'We call decorations "dongles"! We thought we'd go green this year. It's good to get into the festive spirit, don't you think? Do you have dongles at home?'

'Er, no, we have decorations,' said Nelly, 'made from paper or tinsel a bit like this.' She flicked her ponytail round to reveal the purple tinsel she had woven into her scrunchy.

'Weird!' thwucked Lump.

Nelly dropped her gaze from the Dendrilegs' festive ceiling and redirected it to the far corner of the room.

There in the shadows beside the fireplace was something she hadn't noticed on any of her previous visits to the Dendrilegs' home. It was tall and it was green, and from where she was sitting, it looked as though it might just be a Christmas tree.

She took another double bite from her num nums and squinted the full length of the lounge. It was the right shape for a Christmas tree. It was thin enough at the top, broad enough at the bottom, and green enough all over. Except . . .

. . . it was trembling.

Now tall, broad, green Christmas trees she'd seen before. But tall, broad, green Christmas trees that trembled? Never.

'What kind of Christmas tree is that?' she asked, pointing to the shadowy corner beside the fireplace. 'Is it a non-drop, or will you be hoovering up needles into the new year?'

Poltis and Lump looked at each other, and blinked with all eight eyes.

'Christmas tree?' thwucked Poltis. 'Needles on a tree? Where do you get your ideas from! Trees don't grow in houses, they grow outside! Even at Christmas!'

'And it isn't needles that grow on trees, it's leaves!!' laughed Bog and Blotch.

Nelly frowned and did her best to explain.

'In my house we have a Christmas tree at Christmas. A Christmas tree is a tree we put in the house and decorate,' she explained. 'Honestly, it really does have green needles instead of green leaves!'

Lump and Poltis dragged their chairs a little closer to the sofa and tried their hardest not to laugh.

'Except,' continued Nelly, 'sometimes the trees aren't real – they're artificial, made of green plastic or silver tinsel. Like in my scrunchy,' she said, with a flick of her ponytail.

Lump looked at Poltis and snorted.

'We have special Christmas tree dongles,' Nelly continued. 'And Christmas tree lights. And a fairy on the top.'

Poltis looked at Lump, eyes watering.

'It could be a star instead of a fairy – not a real star, a pretend star,' said Nelly, trying to sound as convincing as possible.

But it was no good. The Dendrilegs had lost it.

'Christmas trees indeeeeed!' they spluttered, slipping from their cushions and collapsing on to the hairy carpet in a spaghetti of hysterics. 'In a house! With stars and lights and fairies on top!'

Nelly sighed. Did it really sound that ridiculous?

Maybe they had a point.

'Ooooooooooo Nelly, you are a joker sometimes!' said Poltis, wriggling around on the carpet.

Nelly chuckled, popped the last pieces of num num into her mouth, and switched her attention back to the far end of the room.

OK, if it wasn't a Christmas tree standing in the shadows beside the fireplace, what was it?

It was green all right. And it was definitely a kind of Christmas tree shape, broad at the bottom and pointed at the top, with a triangular outline stretching at least three metres upwards to full ceiling height.

From the look of Lump and Poltis they could be giggling for days. If she wanted to find out, she had two simple choices. She could wait for the Dendrilegs' fit of hysterics to subside, or she could solve the mystery for herself.

Nelly stood up from the sofa, skirted around the heap of wriggling tentacles, and padded across the carpet.

As she drew closer to the chimney breast, the mistake she had made became monstrously clear.

For cowering in the shadows beside the Dendrilegs' chimney breast was a huge green pulsating maggot!

'What on earth is THAT?' gasped Nelly, raising a trembling finger.

Lump, Poltis, Blotch and Bog looked up from the carpet and then collapsed into another heap of squiggles and giggles.

'It's a Gravygrub, of course!' thwucked Poltis.

'A great big fat juicy Gravygrub. Full of lovely green Christmas gravy!'

'What else would someone have beside the fireplace at Christmas?' squealed Lump, with a thwuckery spluck spluck spluck.

'OOOH, it is fun having Nelly here for Christmas! She is SUCH a joker!' thwucked Poltis, dragging herself up from the carpet and squiggling across the room to be by Nelly's side.

'Surely you've seen a Gravygrub before?' thwucked Poltis, slapping two tentacles around Nelly's shoulder and dragging her forward for a close-up look. 'Every monster puts a Gravygrub beside the chimney at Christmas. Surely your family do too?'

Nelly shook her head. 'Actually, we don't!'

'It's fattened up ever so nicely for Christmas,' thwucked Lump, joining Nelly and his wife.

Nelly gasped. 'Do you mean you're going to eat it?'

Lump looked at Poltis, and then collapsed on to the floor like a puppet with its strings cut.

'Of course we're not going to eat it!' spluttered

Lump. 'Dendrilegs don't eat Gravygrubs!'

'Then why's it trembling?' asked Nelly.

'You'll see!' laughed Blotch, her cheeks blue with laughter.

'Yes!' chuckled Bog. 'At nine o'clock, Nelly, you'll see!'

6

It was seven num nums past seven, and Nelly was fast becoming a huge source of amusement for the Dendrilegs.

'Father Who?' thwucked Bog, returning to the settee and nudging Nelly towards the middle cushion.

'Father Christmas,' sighed Nelly, deciding to leave Lump and Poltis out of this conversation.

'I thought your father was called Clifford?' thwucked Blotch, laying claim to Nelly's right knee with a friendly tentacle.

'Father Christmas isn't my father, he's every child's father . . . sort of,' whispered Nelly.

Bog and Blotch stared across Nelly's lap at one another, and then quizzed Nelly some more.

'Does Father Christmas live at your house?' asked Blotch, a little baffled.

'No, he lives in the North Pole in a log cabin with his little elf helpers,' said Nelly. 'He's got a long white beard and he wears a red and white suit, and on Christmas Eve he comes to your house and brings you presents . . . but only if you've been good.'

Bog and Blotch's gummy lips grinned wide.

'You're pulling our tentacles!' laughed Bog.

'I'm not!' insisted Nelly. 'It's true!'

Blotch winked four eyes at her brother.

'How does he know if you've been good?' she giggled.

'He just knows,' said Nelly.

'But HOW?'

Nelly was beginning to struggle now.

'Er . . . he just does. Father Christmas can see all the children in the world all of the time.'

'He must have lots of eyes,' snorted Bog.

'Er no . . . only two,' whispered Nelly, 'but he's got lots of reindeer. When he's delivering presents Father Christmas flies through the sky on a sledge pulled by reindeer. The one at the front is called Rudolph and he's got a red . . .'

Nelly began to falter. Even she thought she was beginning to sound ridiculous now.

'. . . nose.'

Bog and Blotch slipped off the sofa again and collapsed into a goofy-toothed fit of giggles.

'You're soooooooooooo funny!' they thwuck-thwuck spluckety-splucked. 'Please, Nelly, tell it to Mum and Dad!'

Lump and Poltis gazed towards the sofa with quizzical smiles.

'What have you been whispering to the girls about Nelly?' they laughed. 'Not more of your far-fetched Christmas stories!'

Nelly reached for another num num. 'Never mind,' she sighed.

Another fifteen num nums passed by before the Dendrileg twins found the strength to pick themselves up off the carpet.

'A tree with needles on INDEED!' thwucked Bog.

'A Father Christmas INDEED!' wheezed Blotch. 'You'll make us laugh our tentacles off if you're not careful!'

Nelly smiled. 'OK, from now on we'll just talk about your Christmas traditions, not mine. Then there won't be any more misunderstandings. Come on. Who's going to go first?'

But the Dendrilegs were too tickled to let it rest.

'If you want something with needles,' chortled Lump, 'you should drape your fairy lights over a Hojpog!'

'A Hojpog wouldn't stand still for long enough!' laughed Nelly. 'And they don't smell of pine needles.'

'No, we all know what a Hojpog smells of, don't we, kids?' thwucked Poltis, using two tentacles at once to pinch her nose.

'Phewwweeeeeee!' groaned Bog and Blotch, dropping to the carpet in a pretend faint.

Nelly nodded. They were right. Hojpogs were a little on the whiffy side. Especially the ones she'd monster sat in the summer.

'What about Christmas party games?' she suggested, trying to change the subject. 'Do Dendrilegs play party games at Christmas?'

'Oh yes!' thwucked Bog, springing from the floor and yanking Nelly from the sofa. 'Do you know how to play *Earhear*, Nelly? Come on, Mum; come on, Dad; come on, Blotch; let's all play *Earhear*.'

'Thank goodness for that!' thought Nelly. 'Now it's my turn to be entertained!'

7

Nelly watched with interest as Bog took centre stage in the middle of the carpet and lifted himself up on to one tentacle. Poltis, Lump and Blotch moved to the edge of their seats and cocked all four ears in the direction of Bog.

'Earhear,' he said, closing all four eyes and plugging three of his four ears in turn.

Nelly turned to Blotch, Lump and Poltis and watched as they followed suit, plugging ears one, three and four with the rubbery tips of their tentacles.

'Earhear with your second ear,' he thwucked, 'something beginning with T S O B W.'

'I've only got two ears,' said Nelly, unsure whether to cover up one or both.

'Just fill one of them then,' smiled Bog. 'Remember, it's T S O B W.'

Nelly stuck her finger in her right ear, closed her eyes and listened hard.

'THE SOUND OF BLOTCH'S WATCH!' thwucked Poltis triumphantly.

'Correct!' thwucked Bog.

Nelly opened her eyes and found Poltis doing a Christmas victory wiggle on the carpet.

She listened again hard with her left ear, removed her finger from her right ear, and then listened even harder with both. She couldn't hear a thing. She certainly couldn't hear a watch. She looked all the way along Blotch's tentacles. She couldn't even SEE a watch!

'Blotch isn't wearing a watch!' she protested.

'Yes I am!' thwucked Blotch, lifting her new T-shirt to reveal a saucer-sized watch dial belted around her waist by a leopard skin patterned strap.

'I still can't hear it ticking,' said Nelly, giving both ears a good waggle with her fingers.

'Try standing on one leg,' thwucked Blotch. 'You might be able to hear better standing on one leg.'

Nelly looked unsure. In fact she looked downright sceptical. But again, in the spirit of a Dendrilegs Christmas, she decided to play along.

'My turn,' thwucked Poltis, taking centre stage.

'Earhear with your fourth ear,' she thwucked, rising effortlessy up on to one tentacle and then plugging ears number one, two and three in turn, 'something beginning with T S O A G P!'

'The sound of . . .' said Nelly, with a one-legged wobble.

She was halfway there, but the AGP part of the answer was nowhere to be heard. She unplugged her right ear, switched to her left ear but then began to lose her balance.

'A Gravygrub Panicking!' laughed Lump, pointing all his available tentacles in the direction of the fireplace.

'CORRECT!' thwucked Poltis, opening all four eyes and giving her husband some rubbery applause.

Nelly toppled over and put the foot she had lifted up back down on the carpet.

'Gravygrub?' she thought. It was hard enough to SEE the Gravygrub clearly from here, let alone HEAR it clearly! The Dendrilegs must have the hearing of fruit bats!

'Listen to his little hearts going pitterry-patterypoo!' giggled Blotch. 'He's getting nerrrrvous!'

'I'm not surprised!' laughed Blotch, lifting her T-shirt to peer at her watch. It was almost a quarter to eight.

'NEARLY TIME,' thwucked Blotch.

Nelly frowned. The Dendrilegs could hear a pin *fall*, let alone drop!

She pulled her finger out of her ear and sighed. To win at a game like *Earhear* she would need to use both her ears and borrow two more from an African elephant.

'My turn!' thwucked Blotch, eager not to be left out.

'I think I'll sit this one out,' smiled Nelly, returning to the sofa. 'If you hear a crunch, it will be the sound of another Num Num.'

Lump and Poltis laughed, and waited lovingly

for their daughter to assume the single tentacle position.

'Earhear with your first . . . no, second . . . no, fourth . . .'

'We've done fourth,' thwucked Bog, unplugging three ears in rapid succession.

'Third, I meant,' thwucked Blotch. 'Earhear with your third ear, something beginning with . . .'

Blotch listened hard and then by way of a clue cocked her head in the direction of the kitchen. 'T S O C!'

Nelly turned her head towards the kitchen door and frowned. The sound of C? Cutlery? Cornflakes? Chips? Chipolatas? Chocolate sauce? Corkscrew?

'You have them at Christmas,' thwucked Bog.

Nelly turned back to the Dendrilegs. Everyone had guessed it.

'They're green,' said Blotch.

'It's obvious!' chuckled Bog.

Nelly began to feel a little bit stupid. She nibbled her lip. The sound of C? Coming from the kitchen? C? Crumbs? Cauliflower? Carrots? Casserole dish? Cettle? Perhaps not . . .

'You find them in a box!' said Lump.

'You pull them!' thwucked Poltis.

'Crackers!' shouted Nelly.

The Dendrilegs slapped their tentacles together, applauded momentarily and then frowned.

'You mean croakers,' thwucked Poltis.

'Here we go again,' sighed Nelly.

8

CHRISTMAS CRACKER: *A cardboard tube from a loo roll wrapped in coloured crêpe paper, with a useless joke, cheap plastic toy, party hat, rubber band and cracker snap inside. Pulled by two people before or during Christmas dinner.*

CHRISTMAS CROAKER: *A green croaking frog's head with two croaking mouths and a pair of slimy frog's legs either end. Pink explosive powder and a festive hologram inside. Pulled by two monsters or more before, during or after Christmas dinner.*

When the box of Christmas croakers first landed on Nelly's lap, she didn't know whether to smile politely or simply squirm. The box itself was plain enough: red in colour and about twice the size and length of a normal cracker box. It had rigid plastic sides and a glass viewing window in the lid.

Viewing, however, wasn't easy because white bubbling froth had collected on the underside of the glass, obscuring the croakers inside.

'Shall we pull some?' thwucked Lump.

'YEEESSSSSSSSSSS!!!!!!!' chorused the twins.

Nelly gulped. The froth beneath the glass was bubbling from a line of green gaping mouths. And although the mouths seemed to be smiling, she wasn't at all convinced that the contents were entirely happy. She lowered one ear to the glass lid and listened hard. As far as she could make out, there were no croaks to be heard. At least not with the two human ears she had at her disposal.

Poltis lifted the box from Nelly's lap and whipped off the lid. 'Come on, everybody,' she thwucked, 'it's Christmas croaker time!'

As the soundproof seal of the croaker lid broke, the lounge began to reverberate with the loud foghorning honk of bullfrogs. Nelly put her hands over her ears and shuddered as Bog plucked a croaker from the box and thrust a pair of webbed feet forward for her to pull.

She stared at the glistening mottled legs. They

reminded her a little uncomfortably of the Water Greeps.

With a grimace and a shudder she closed the palm of her right hand around the cold and slimy webbing and squeezed the two croaker feet together as hard as she dared.

'One, two, three, PULL!' thwucked Bog, yanking his croaker legs clean off from the body and squealing in delight as a puff of pink smoke billowed into the air.

Nelly looked down at her clenched fist. She hadn't quite mustered the courage to pull hard enough. As a result she had been left

holding two lifeless croaker legs dangling from a croakless body.

'Watch, Nelly! Watch!' thwucked Bog, lobbing his detonated croaker legs over the back of the sofa and grabbing another croaker from the box.

Nelly looked up at the small cloud of pink mist, and then gasped as it suddenly faded away to be replaced by the hologram of a Gravygrub trembling beside a chimney breast.

'They're not all holograms of Gravygrubs,' thwucked Bog. 'There are seven different Christmas designs in every box!'

Nelly turned her head towards Blotch, Poltis and Lump. Amid the furore of croaks, squeals and thwucks, a much larger cloud of pink smoke had mushroomed over the settee.

Eighteen quizzical eyes settled on the smoke as it suddenly evaporated to reveal the hologram of a leopard-spotted, three-headed, jelly-shelled sort of tortoise spinning upside down on a plate.

'Carrilope! We eat those for breakfast on Christmas morning!' thwucked Lump. 'You should try some, Nelly – you'd love them.

Especially in a great big bowl of Leru milk!'

Nelly nodded uncertainly and then wiped some croaker slime discreetly on to the leg of her new Christmas jeans.

'Let's pull the last five all together!' laughed Blotch, shepherding everyone into a circle.

Nelly put her unexploded croaker legs down on the arm of the sofa and braced herself to receive another pair.

Two pairs, in fact. One in her outstretched left hand, where Poltis had joined the circle, and the other in her right, where Lump was standing.

'Now remember to pull harder this time, Nelly,' thwucked Bog, tentacles and croaker at the ready. 'If you don't pull hard enough, the legs won't explode properly!'

Nelly nodded grimly and joined in the countdown from five to BANG.

And quite a bang it was. About as loud as a one-barrel shot-gun.

Nelly jumped, and then shuddered. She had certainly pulled hard enough this time. Two pairs of lifeless amphibian croaker legs dangled from each clenched fist now. Slime was dripping slowly down from the knobble of each kneebone and sizzling at the detached part where each leg was still smoking.

'Look, Nelly! Look at all the different Christmas things that have come out of the croakers!' clapped Blotch. 'That's a Peelywizz, that's a Breeeeem, that's a Longbell, and that's a Zoody's heelpipper!'

Nelly looked into the middle of the circle and gazed at the pink misty mirage of monster holograms floating before her eyes. There were things that looked like birds, birds that looked like things, shapes that reshaped themselves, objects that squirmed and something even a dictionary doesn't have the vocabulary for.

'We don't have stuff like that at Christmas,' winced Nelly. 'We have normal stuff like baubles and crackers and robins and snowmen.'

'Tell us more!' thwucked Poltis, anticipating some more of Nelly's hilarious Christmas stories.

'Oh no,' smiled Nelly. 'I don't want you laughing your tentacles off at me!'

302

She went to put her croaker legs down on the arm of the sofa and then suddenly wheeled around. A moment of inspiration had struck her. With a sweep of her arm she motioned to the Dendrileg family to form a circle again.

'OK, everyone, pick up your croaker legs and follow me!'

Bog, Blotch, Lump and Poltis watched with interest as Nelly broke out into a peculiar, but rather interesting, song and dance.

'DA DA DA DA DA DA . . .

YOU PUT YOUR RIGHT TENTACLE IN,
YOUR RIGHT TENTACLE OUT,
IN OUT,
IN OUT,
SHAKE IT ALL ABOUT.
YOU DO THE OKEY CROAKY AND YOU
TURN AROUND.
THAT'S WHAT IT'S ALL ABOUT!

'JOIN HANDS, EVERYONE!' Nelly cried, turning full circle on the spot and then swinging her croaker legs into the air for Lump and Bog to latch hold of.

'WOOAAH, THE OKEY CROAKY!' she sang, dragging Bog and Lump into the middle of the circle and then back again.

'WOOAAH, THE OKEY CROAKY!
WOOAAH, THE OKEY CROAKY!
KNEES BEND, TENTACLES STRETCH,
RAH RAH RAH!'

Blotch, Bog, Lump and Poltis stared at one another, and then rippled from top to toe with excitement.

'I thought you said you didn't have croakers at home, Nelly!' thwucked Lump.

'We don't,' smiled Nelly.

'Then how do you know a croaker dance?'

'I kind of made it up!' laughed Nelly. 'Are you ready for Verse TWO?'

The Dendrilegs were more than ready for Verse Two. With croakers at the ready and tentacles poised, they waited for Nelly to give the sign.

'LEFT TENTACLES THIS TIME!' she shouted, pointing her left trainer forward and then setting off on another burst of Okey Croaky.

She was on to a Christmas winner. The Dendrilegs danced and sang along with gusto, swinging their croaker legs high in the air like Morris dancers' handkerchiefs and strutting their tentacles like Cossacks.

'THIS IS MORE FUN THAN EARHEAR!' thwucked Blotch, putting her third tentacle in and out.

'This is the BEST!' laughed Bog, putting his whole self, and then his fourth tentacle, in by mistake.

In they went, out they went, doing the Okey Croaky and turning around and around and around.

It was an Okey Croaking twenty-two encores before the friends finally collapsed into a heap on the floor.

'I'm all croaked out,' gasped Nelly.

'Me toooooo!' thwucked Lump.

'That was brilliant!' wheezed Blotch, lobbing

her croaker legs over the back of the sofa. 'From now on, we must do the Okey Croaky every Christmas!'

'My nan taught me how to do it when I was little,' panted Nelly, lobbing her croaker legs a little too hard and sending them sliding down the French window curtains. 'I think everyone should do it every day!'

Poltis and Lump raised themselves up from the carpet, and discarded their croaker legs over the back of the sofa too.

'I think it's time for some more Christmas refreshments,' thwucked Lump. 'Can we get you something to drink, Nelly?'

'Demonade, please,' said Nelly. 'If you've got any, that is.'

'Purple or brown?' asked Poltis, wiggle-waggling her way through to the kitchen.

'Purple, please,' said Nelly, sticking with the flavour she'd already tried and loved at the Muggots'.

'I'll bring some Nibnobs in too,' said Poltis. 'I'm afraid my homemade churly freeps didn't come out too well. Too much yelk yolk in the mix, I think.'

Nelly scrambled back on to the sofa, and dropped like a sack of potatoes into the cushions. She was exhausted.

And then sandwiched by the attentions of Bog and Blotch.

'Move up a bit!' thwucked Bog. 'Remember, if you're in the middle then it will be fair.'

Nelly obliged, and then placed her arms around the shoulders of each twin in turn.

'Tell us another funny Christmas story,' thwucked Bog.

Nelly smiled and shook her head. 'No way!'

'That Gravygrub seems to be trembling even more now!' she frowned, peering towards the shadowy corner beside the chimney breast.

Blotch glanced at the fireplace and then lifted her T-shirt to look down at her watch. It was twenty past eight.

'No wonder!' she thwucked. 'Only forty minutes to go, Nelly! Only forty minutes to the big surprise. Hooray! Here come the Nibnobs!'

9

Nelly loosened the top button of her jeans. The Okey Croaky had shaken up all the num nums she had eaten and now a bowl of Nibnobs was being wafted in front of her face.

'I couldn't possibly,' she fibbed, plunging her fingers into the white Formica bowl and removing a fistful of the little blue sticks.

'I love Nibnobs,' thwucked Blotch, grabbing two tentacles full for herself.

'Here's your demonade, Nelly,' thwucked Poltis, handing Nelly a tall frosted glass of purple frothy liquid.

'Many thanks,' said Nelly, taking the glass with her free hand and then tipping her head back to pop some Nibnobs into her mouth.

'MMMM! Delish!' she munched, as the caramel-flavoured sticks splintered between her teeth.

Bog, Blotch, Lump and Poltis looked at each other curiously and then carried their own glasses of demonade over to where Nelly was sitting.

Nelly paused in mid-crunch and looked down at her palm full of Nibnobs, then up at sixteen enquiring eyes.

'What?' she said.

'You're not meant to do that with them,' thwucked Blotch, sprinkling some of her Nibnobs into her glass of demonade. 'Their legs won't grow if you eat them like that.'

Nelly turned white and swallowed dryly.

Blotch held out her glass of demonade for Nelly to see.

'If their legs don't grow, they can't swim to the bottom of the glass,' explained Poltis.

'And if they don't swim to the bottom of the glass, they can't turn the bubbles into cubes,' thwucked Lump.

'Square bubbles are fizzier than round bubbles,' nodded Blotch.

Nelly eased forward and peered into the Dendrilegs' glasses of demonade. The sky blue

Nibnobs they had sprinkled on to the surface had sprouted three pairs of pink water boatman legs. Not only that, they were canoeing across the froth that foamed at the top of the glass.

'Watch what they do now,' thwucked Poltis.

Nelly's eyes saucered wide as one by one each Nibnob barrel rolled through the froth and dived like a submarine to the bottom of Bog's glass.

'Here comes the FIZZ!' squealed Bog with an excited suckery thwuck.

The Dendrilegs braced themselves in turn as one by one their glasses erupted like purple volcanoes.

'Quick! Before it overflows!' thwucked Blotch, slapping her rubbery lips to the rim of her glass and downing the demonade in one.

Bog, Poltis and Lump followed suit, draining their glasses in quick succession and then wiping their tentacles across their mouths.

'THAT'S WHAT YOU DO WITH NIBNOBS, NELLY!' laughed Blotch.

Nelly dropped the rest of her Nibnobs back into the bowl and shuddered. She'd eaten insects! She'd eaten a whole mouthful of them like they were a handful of peanuts! She shuddered again. How well had she chewed them? Well enough or not quite well enough? Had she chewed them dead? Or could some of them still be alive and well, about to sprout legs inside her stomach and go for a long paddle through her gastric juices?

Putting on the bravest face she could manage, she raised her glass of demonade to her lips and smiled.

'Cheers!' she said, deciding that the best course of action would be to flush the chewed-up Nibnobs as far down as possible.

'You DO do some funny things, Nelly!' laughed Bog. 'Fancy eating Nibnobs at Christmas!'

Nelly forced a smile as the Dendrilegs tipped the Nibnobs from their glasses and stamped them into the carpet.

'I did say I hadn't tried Nibnobs before, Lump!' she protested. 'You could have told me I wasn't meant to eat them!'

'Oh yes, you did tell me, didn't you?' said

Lump absent-mindedly. 'Sorry, Nelly. Next time I'll remind you.'

'I won't need reminding next time, thank you!' said Nelly, flopping back on to the sofa. She wasn't sure there would be a next time either!

Lump raised a tentacle up to the ceiling and slapped a dongle like a punchball. 'Nelly's so hungry on Christmas Day, she's taken to eating insects!' he laughed.

'Poltis, if Nelly's that hungry, then I think we might have just the thing for her to eat. Come and help me carry it in!'

Nelly puffed out her cheeks and loosened another button on her jeans. 'Please, no more to eat!' she protested. 'I couldn't eat an ant! I've already had a big Christmas dinner today, and Christmas pud with custard, and half a box of dates, and all those num nums!'

But it was no use. Poltis and Lump had already wiggle-waggled their way through the door of the kitchen.

'Promise us you'll try one of our mince pies, Nelly!' they thwucked.

At least that's what Nelly thought they had thwucked.

'Oh, all right then,' she groaned, not wanting to appear impolite.

Easing further back into the sofa cushions, she looked left and right. For the first time that evening Bog and Blotch seemed less concerned with claiming a share of her knees and more interested in the Gravygrub.

'It's twenty to nine, Nelly!' thwucked Blotch, lifting her T-shirt and twisting her tummy round for Nelly to view the time on her watch. 'Look at that silly old Gravygrub – he's shaking like a jelly!'

'He knows it's nearly time too!' thwucked Bog, clapping his tentacles together excitedly.

'Time for what?' asked Nelly. 'Come on, Blotch; come on, Bog', she whispered. 'You can tell me!'

Blotch and Bog shook their heads and grinned broad and goofy-toothed smiles.

'No way, Nelly! It's a surpriiiiiiiiiiiiiiiiiiiiiiise!'

10

Nelly settled back into the sofa. She hadn't really expected them to spill the beans, but it was worth a try.

With a playful squeeze of the twins' tentacles, she turned her head away from the Gravygrub and peered over the back of the sofa. A series of loud huffs, puffs, grunts and groans were coming from the kitchen.

A purple shoulder and tentacle appeared briefly in the kitchen doorway but then disappeared almost as quickly. Back it came. Away it went. There were some more huffs, some more puffs, and some rather rubbery rasps.

Then squeak by squeak, rasp by rasp, Lump and Poltis began to emerge through the doorway, arms full, tentacles flexed and cheeks puffing to bursting point.

Nelly turned round to face the kitchen, and watched in astonishment as the two adult Dendrilegs manoeuvred their way awkwardly into the lounge. They looked like removal men trying to carry in a heavy wardrobe.

Except it wasn't a wardrobe they were carrying. It was a pie.

A pie the size of a dustbin lid.

'It was freshly baked yesterday!' thwucked Poltis proudly. 'Tuck in, you hungry girl!'

Nelly gritted her teeth as Lump and Poltis shuffled like overloaded pensioners around the back of the sofa. Surely it wasn't a pie for one?

'It's a bit heavy,' thwucked Lump, attempting to wipe his brow with one tentacle but then deciding to hold on with everything he could.

'It's made with self-sinking flour,' gasped Poltis. 'If this doesn't fill you up, nothing will!'

Nelly sat rooted between the twins, and braced herself for the arrival of a two-tonne piece of pastry.

'Here it comes!' thwucked Lump, staggering

with his wife towards the sofa. 'Get your teeth into this, Nelly!'

Nelly's eyes bulged and her knees sank deep into the sofa cushions as the Dendrilegs heaved the giant pie on to her lap. It was heavy all right. The moment it landed on her lap Nelly felt the aluminium pie dish buckling softly

around her knees. She tried to move her legs, but she was trapped.

'I thought you said "mince" pie,' she gulped.

'In my house we have mince pies at Christmas.'

'In our house we have Immense Pies at Christmas!' wheezed Lump.

Nelly peered down at the giant pastry crust. It wasn't charcoal black like her mum's homemade pastry, it was glazed a beautiful golden yellow.

She gave it a sniff. It didn't smell of bonfires like her mum's homemade pastry, it had the rather spicy smell of curry and fresh chillies.

'Tuck in, Nelly!' thwucked Poltis. 'Don't be shy!'

Nelly smiled sweetly, reached forward and closed her fingers around the lip of the golden pastry crust. With a squeeze of her fingers and a twist of her wrist, she prised a large fistful of pastry from the pie dish.

The spicy chilli smell grew stronger as she raised it to her lips.

'What's the pastry made of?' she asked cautiously, determined not to swallow any more insects – or insect flavouring, for that matter.

'Just flour, Leru milk and yelk yolks,' thwucked Poltis. 'It's a classic Christmas recipe!'

Nelly closed her eyes and sank her teeth into the pastry. They closed softly together and then stuck fast.

'Don't worry,' thwucked Poltis, reading the surprise in Nelly's eyes. 'That's the self-sinking flour. It will dissolve in a moment! Then you'll get the real flavour of the pastry!'

Nelly waited patiently for the flour to dissolve and her teeth to unlock, then she raised her thumb in approval as the taste of spicy sausage and onions flooded on to her tongue.

'It's delicious!' she smiled. 'My compliments to the chef!'

Poltis beamed proudly and then pointed at the pie with two of her tentacles. 'You haven't tried the filling yet!' she thwucked.

Nelly blew out her cheeks. She was full to bursting after just one mouthful of pie crust. How on earth was she going to dig into the filling?

But dig in she did – quite literally, using her outstretched fingers as a shovel.

As her fingernails broke through the surface of the pastry, she didn't really know what to expect.

What she got were goldfish. At least that's what it felt like: a pie stuffed with cold, dead goldfish.

'Queels,' thwucked Poltis before Nelly could ask the question. 'Sugared Queels. A real Christmas favourite in our house, Nelly, but watch out for the bones and leave the beaks on the arm of the sofa. We'll throw them in the bin later.'

Nelly looked down at the one half of her forearm still visible above the hole in the pastry crust. She stroked her fingers blindly across the small scaly back of an ingredient hidden inside. Somehow, not being able to see what she had been invited to eat made it all the less appetizing. She inched her fingertips a little further along. Was that a beak she could feel or a fin?

All sixteen Dendrileg eyes fastened excitedly on to Nelly as slowly and unsurely she pulled a fistful of filling from the pie.

As her hand re-emerged from the pastry crust a strangely floral scent rose from the hole she had shovelled into. Nelly sniffed. It reminded her of the lavender air freshener they had in the loo at home.

With as convincing a smile as she could muster, she lifted her hand to mouth height and gingerly opened her fingers.

There in the palm of her hand was something that like a sugar-frosted duckbilled goldfish. It had been roasted in a curled-up position with a sprig of lavender inserted into each gill. Its scales were glazed candyfloss pink and its fins were singed black.

'Yuk!' thought Nelly.

'Tuck in!' thwucked Bog.

'Yes, sugared Queels are yum,' thwucked Blotch.

Nelly shuddered. She needed an escape plan and she needed one fast.

'If I eat all this, I'll be fatter than that Gravygrub!' she protested.

'GRAVYGRUB!' thwucked Lump in a panic. 'What time is it? I'D COMPLETELY FORGOTTEN THE TIME!'

To Nelly's utter amazement and huge, huge relief, pandemonium suddenly broke out in the Dendrilegs' lounge.

'Quick!' thwucked Lump, leaping from his armchair and pointing his tentacles in all directions at once. 'Open all the windows!'

'Yes, open all the windows,' thwucked Poltis. 'It's almost five to nine!'

Bog and Blotch sprang from Nelly's side and raced round the back of the sofa to open the French windows.

'I'll do upstairs!' thwucked Lump.

'I'll do the lounge and the kitchen!' thwucked Poltis.

With the Dendrilegs at sixes and sevens, Nelly seized the opportunity to press the sugared Queel back inside the pie.

'I hope they didn't notice,' she phewed, as the stampede of tentacles broke out before her.

But she needn't have worried. If she'd thrown the Queel into the middle of the lounge carpet, they would have been oblivious.

'Where's the key to the window locks!' thwucked Lump from the top of the stairs.'

'In the Purly Pot behind our bed!' shouted Poltis.

Nelly sat confused and motionless, anchored fast to the sofa by the weight of the Immense Pie. Christmas Day at the Dendrilegs' had suddenly exploded into all-action mayhem. In every room of the house, from top to bottom, curtains were being thrown back and windows were being thrown open. But why? It was Christmas madness.

It was a bit chilly too!

An icy December blast blew across the carpet of the Dendrilegs' lounge, sending goosebumps upwards from Nelly's ankle socks.

She shivered. What on earth were the Dendrilegs up to?

Why on earth were they opening all the windows?

She looked at her watch.

It was surprise time.

11

'I like your blouse, Nelly,' puffed Poltis, with the uneasy wheeze of someone who had just completed a half marathon.

'Yes, we like your blouse!' wheezed Lump. 'Did you get it for Christmas?'

With every window in the house thrown wide open, the Dendrilegs had returned to their seats in the lounge and were now trying to act as if nothing had happened at all.

Nelly looked down at her blouse, and then folded her arms across the lid of the Immense Pie. 'Never mind my blouse,' she said. 'Why have you opened all the windows?'

'No reason,' thwucked Lump. 'We just thought you might like a bit of fresh air.'

Fresh air? It was like sitting in a wind tunnel!

Nelly looked suspiciously at the twins

seated innocently on either side of her. Uncharacteristically for them, they were sitting with their tentacles politely crossed and their backs straight.

Nelly tried to shift her legs, but the Immense Pie dish had folded itself like an aluminium blanket around her knees.

'Come on, you lot!' she laughed, rubbing her hands together to keep warm. 'If it's surprise time, at least give me a clue where to look!'

Blotch and Bog's eyes flashed from the ceiling to the chimney breast, giving Nelly her first and only clue.

Nelly stared at the open hearth of the fireplace and then darted her eyes right, in the direction of the Gravygrub. The cold air circulating through the house seemed to have triggered the giant maggot into a bout of uncontrollable shivers.

'He's shaking like a jelly!' gasped Nelly. 'What's the matter with him? Doesn't he like the cold?'

'You'll see!' giggled Bog, moving excitedly to the edge of the sofa and training her four sparkling orange eyes on the chimney breast.

Nelly looked quizzically at each Dendrileg in turn. All sixteen eyes were now rooted to the chimney breast. All sixteen eyes were shining bright as Bethlehem stars.

'Earhear with both of your ears, Nelly,' giggled Blotch, 'something beginning with CC!'

Nelly sat fast and frowned.

She listened hard.

She listened harder.

She listened harder still.

But it was no use. The only thing she could hear was the silence of the deserted street outside.

She stared the full length of the carpet at the shadowy figure of the Gravygrub. It was out of control now, shaking like a Pekinese dog in a snowstorm.

'WE can hear it, Nelly! Can't we, everyone?' thwucked Bog, staring at the chimney breast with a broad, gummy smile.

'Oh yes!' thwucked Lump, Poltis and Blotch, inching closer to the edge of their seats and nodding in the same direction. 'The Gravygrub can hear it too!'

Nelly gave up on her ears and tried inching closer to the edge of her seat. 'It's gone nine o'clock by my watch,' she smiled, raising her wrist and then placing her forearm back down on the pie crust.

'Not by mine!' thwucked Blotch. 'I make it ten seconds to go!'

The Dendrilegs daughter lifted her T-shirt excitedly and turned her watch face in all directions. 'Eight, seven, six . . . !'

Nelly began to tingle. She liked surprises, especially monster ones.

With a clap of her hands, she joined in with the Dendrilegs' Christmas countdown. 'Five!' she smiled.

'Four!' she clapped.

'Three!' she chuckled.

'Two!' she giggled.

'ONE!' she screamed.

Nelly's feet back-pedalled towards the sofa and her jaws locked tight with horror as a pair of giant red pincers suddenly speared downwards from the darkness of the chimney breast and thrust themselves upwards into the lounge.

The pincers rolled from left to right to shake the soot from their steely tips, and then probed the hearth blindly.

Nelly gasped as the leathery white folds of a monstrous insect head began to ooze into view. The folds rippled and peeled back slowly to reveal the coal-black gleam of two giant probing eyes.

'What is it?' she squealed, her legs anchored fast to the sofa by the Immense Pie.

Whatever it was, it was still coming, oozing, squeezing and now scrabbling into the lounge from the tunnel of the chimney flue. Nelly squirmed. Two giant claws were trying to emerge too!

Cramped by the confines of the flue, they scrabbled and scraped against the stone chimney walls, but then slowly and surely they began to lever themselves down.

Nelly stiffened as the first pair of segmented legs sprang open like crimson penknife blades.

Probing the stone hearth with lunges and stabs they moved forward and speared hard down on to the carpet.

With a convulsive surge, and a screeching 'HEE HEE HEE!' the second of a hundred segments oozed into view.

'Centi Claws!' cheered Blotch and Bog, waving their tentacles excitedly in the air and then wriggling from the sofa to greet the visitor.

'How do you like your surprise, Nelly? Come and say hello to Centi Claws!'

Nelly wasn't going anywhere. She was fixed to the sofa by a two-tonne piece of pastry. And had she not been, she would have been out of the open French windows and home!

Her eyes widened to the size of turkey dishes. A snow-white giant centipede with Santa-red legs was crawling down the chimney into the Dendrilegs' lounge! It was huge, it was humongous, and it was coming her way.

Nelly gripped the aluminium pie dish for dear life as body segment after body segment oozed into the room.

The Dendrilegs at Christmas

As each pair of claws squeezed free of the confines of the chimney flue, the leathery white segment they were attached to expanded to the size of an armchair. Nelly watched dumbfounded as the lounge filled with segments and claws.

'It won't hurt you, Nelly!' thwucked Bog, running right up close to the Centi Claws and throwing her tentacles adoringly around the creature's glutinous waistline. 'It's come for its Christmas Gravygrub!'

Nelly shuddered. Any moment now, one hundred rippling segments of Centi Claws would be passing her way!

'We all love Centi Claws, don't we, children?' thwucked Lump, removing a large glass cruet from under the cushion he was sitting on and shaking the contents vigorously over the Gravygrub.

As the grains of something pink bounced from the emerald folds of the Gravygrub's skin, the maggot rigid with fear.

And with good reason. The entire Dendrilegs family had broken out into a raucous round of tentacle-clapping and Gravygrub-chanting.

'Gravygrub! Gravygrub!' they chanted, slapping their tentacles joyously together and stomping them into the hairy carpet.

'Come on, Nelly! Join in!' thwucked Blotch. 'Gravygrub! Gravygrub!'

Nelly gulped in two directions at once. She had one eye on the Gravygrub in the far corner of the room, and the other on a giant centipede that was crawling closer to her with every second.

With a superhuman effort, she struggled and strained to try and free her legs from the weight of the Immense Pie. But it was no use. There was no escape. She wasn't going anywhere.

The Centi Claws was. Ten pairs of articulated legs had emerged from the chimney now, and the hulk of its leathery white body had almost obscured the chimney breast from view.

Nelly had completely lost sight of the Dendrilegs. She knew where they were, and she could still hear them chanting 'Gravygrub! Gravygrub!' but somehow she couldn't help feeling just that little bit alone.

'It won't hurt me!' she thought. 'It won't hurt

me,' she reassured herself, trying to remain as calm as possible as the Centi Claws' gleaming red legs crawled closer to her knees.

Crimson pincers were looming large now and a green gummy mouth was gaping wide. Nelly looked anxiously across the top of the Immense Pie and stared deep into the twinkle of the Centi Claws' eyes.

Her heart skipped a beat.

Twinkle?

She stared closer.

Yes, there most definitely was a twinkle in both eyes!

'Say, HA HA HA, Nelly!' laughed Blotch from the far corner of the room.

'What?' squeaked Nelly.

'Say Ha ha ha!' laughed Bog. 'He likes it if you say Ha ha ha!'

'Ha ha ha!' squeaked Nelly, barely able to get her vocal cords to function.

'HEE HEE HEE!' screeched the Centi Claws, banana-ing its green gummy lips into a broad and friendly smile.

Nelly's legs turned to unset jelly as the Centi Claws' pincers drew centimetres from her nose.

'Hello, Mr Centi Claws,' she smiled. 'Happy Christmas. My name's Nelly. Would you care for an Immense Pie? I'm told they are delicious!'

Nelly stared at her terrorstruck reflection in one of the Centi Claws' eyeballs, and then shut her eyes tight as the Centi Claws its jaws opened wide.

It was all over in a second.

With one humongous chomp of its jaws, the Immense Pie and aluminium dish were gone.

Nelly opened her eyes and stared down at her empty lap. With the weight of the Immense Pie lifted, her knees were rising like freshly baked bread.

'Gravygrub, Gravygrub!' chorused the Dendrilegs from the far corner of the room.

Overcome with the joy of not being eaten, Nelly clapped her hands together with the Dendrilegs and joined in with the chant.

'Gravygrub! Gravygrub! Gravygrub!'

A long brown lizard's tongue flicked from the

Centi Claws' mouth, despatching two Immense Pie crumbs from either side of its mouth. Then with a twinkle of its eyes and a twist of its head, a dozen wriggling body segments wheeled round in the direction of the chimney breast.

Botch and Bog jumped into the air with excitement.

'Here comes Centi Claws! Here comes Centi Claws! La la la la!' they sang.

Nelly eased herself up from the sofa, waited for the blood to circulate through her legs, and then skirted around the Centi Claws' giant body.

She could see the Gravygrub. It was standing stiff as an ironing board beside the chimney breast, trembling like a prisoner awaiting execution.

Mercy of mercies, it didn't have to wait long.

With a loud screeching 'HEE HEE HEE!' the Centi Claws' pincers opened wide and then snapped fast around the Gravygrub's waist. The pincers closed, the Gravygrub's body popped, and green gravy exploded over the wall.

'HOOORRRRAYYYYY!' clapped the Dendrilegs,

flicking spatters of green goo from their tentacles.

With a slithering suck, the green gummy gums of the Centi Claws' cavernous jaws hoovered up the saggy remains of the Gravygrub's carcass and it then set about licking the walls clean with its tongue.

'Isn't he wonderful?' thwucked Blotch, running to Nelly's side and slapping a tentacle around her waist.

'Did you like your surprise, Nelly?' laughed Bog, wiping a splash of green gravy from his chest. 'Is it your best Christmas surprise ever?'

Nelly nodded her head. 'It certainly is,' she smiled, not quite sure whether to feel sorry for the Gravygrub or not.

A circle of Dendrileg tentacles corralled Nelly tighter into their midst and sixteen smiling Dendrileg eyes closed in for a whisper.

'Now get ready for Surprise Number Two!'

12

'You'd best wear your coat,' said Lump, handing Nelly her Puffa jacket.

Nelly took her coat from Lump's outstretched tentacle and watched as the Centi Claws U-turned away from the fireplace and scurried back in the direction of the open double doors.

'Where's it going?' asked Nelly, flattening herself against the wall as the legs of the humongous insect scurried past her like marching soldiers.

'Up down and all around!' smiled Blotch, as the Centi Claws departed from the lounge through the open French windows.

Nelly stood transfixed as segment after segment of skirrying scurrying legs beetled into the garden, U-turned through the kitchen window, wound their way through the

Dendrilegs' kitchen door, back into the lounge and through the doorway leading to the hall.

'Centi Claws is going upstairs now,' clapped Bog.

'He'll be back down in a few minutes!' laughed Lump.

Nelly gasped. The Centi Claws was threading itself through the house like a shoelace.

'Here he comes!' giggled Blotch, tugging Nelly by the elbow and turning her round to face the open bay window at the front of the house.

To Nelly's bewilderment, the twinkling coal-black eyes of the Centi Claws were about to pass by her again! Having squeezed through the downstairs doorway of the hall, its sinuous snaking body had climbed the stairs, turned out of an upstairs window, and looped downwards through the night sky. It was like watching a tube train pass by. Only this was a tube train with legs!

Back through the open bay window it came, then out through the open French window, and still more and more segments were emerging from the chimney!

Nelly ran into the back garden and tipped her head back to look two storeys up to the roofline of the house. Twisting and turning like a skyscraping anaconda, the Centi Claws' body had circled the house twice before threading itself back indoors through an upstairs bedroom window.

'Bathroom window next!' clapped Bog.

'Then the roof!' thwucked his sister.

Nelly watched and then clapped as the giant twinkling smile of the Centi Claws looped into view from the open bathroom window and then swept sideways through an open bedroom window.

'It's like a magical tube of never-ending toothpaste!' laughed Nelly. 'No it isn't,' she clapped. 'I'll tell you what it's like – it's like a big dipper!'

'All aboard!' cheered Bog and Blotch, wrapping their tentacles around Nelly's sleeve and tugging her back into the lounge.

Nelly stumbled in through the open French windows and turned her attention to the fireplace.

'Just in time,' thwucked Blotch excitedly as the one hundredth and final segment of the Centi Claws' body dropped down from the chimney breast and ballooned like an armchair into view.

Like all the segments that had looped their way through the house before it, the final segment was snow-white too, with giant Santa-red legs attached. However, this segment was a segment with a difference.

Nelly's pulse yo-yoed.

The final segment of the Centi Claws' body had seating inside!

'Climb in quickly, Nelly,' thwucked Bog, 'before Centi Claws leaves without us! There's plenty of room for three!'

Nelly stood slack-armed and open-jawed as the sloping leathery bonnet of the carriage pulled up beside her. The back of the segment sloped upwards like a dodgem car, and from each corner, giant insect feelers wobbled like car aerials.

'Quick, Nelly!' thwucked Bog as the aerials began to flash like fireflies. 'Quick or you'll miss out on the ride!'

Nelly took charge of her senses and scrambled into the space beside the twins.

'In the middle, Nelly! In the middle, remember! Then it will be fair!' thwucked Blotch.

Nelly obliged as quickly as she could, clambering over Bog's rubbery tentacles and taking her place between the twins.

'Have fun!' waved Poltis and Lump from their corner beside the fireplace.

'You'll be dropped off at your home!' thwucked Lump, stepping back as the antennae lights began to glow green. 'Thanks ever so much for coming to visit us, Nelly. We hope you liked your Christmas surprises!'

Even Nelly's tingles were tingling now. Was what she thought was about to happen REALLY about to happen?

It was.

With a shudder and a clunk, the rear segment of the Centi Claws' body shunted forward like a fairground carriage. Nelly stared straight ahead and then sat bolt upright as three pairs of silver safety claws sprang down from behind her, pinning all three friends securely into position.

'Here we gooooooooooooooooooooo!' whooped Blotch. 'Happy Christmas, Nelllllllllyyy!'

Nelly gripped the twins' tentacles as the rear segment shunted forward again, but this time with more momentum.

Nelly looked left and right at the giant claws that were propelling their carriage. The claws were scurrying now, drawing them across the hairy carpet towards the open French window doors. Nelly grinned at the girls seated on either side of her. If only her school mates could see her now!

The Centi Claws' legs began to rise and fall with the rhythm and power of a steam engine. Like pistons they rose and fell.

'HEEE HEEEE!' whistled the front carriage.

'Ha ha ha!' shouted the twins.

Nelly leaned back and raised her arms in the air. They were out through the French window doors now and into the garden!

The cold December air frosted her cheeks as

the Centi Claws' big-dipping body surged on to the lawn and U-turned sharply backwards through the open kitchen window.

'Don't forget to wave to Mum and Dad, Nelly,' said Blotch. 'We'll be going back through the lounge in a moment!'

'Arms down, Nelly!' laughed Bog as they burst back into the house through the window.

Nelly dropped her arms in the nick of time and then lurched sideways as they careered over the kitchen units and back into the lounge.

'Hi, Mum! Hi, Dad!' waved the twins as a twisting spiralling sharp turn sent them hurtling into the hallway.

Nelly tried to catch a glimpse of Lump and Poltis, but she had barely lifted her hand to wave before she was hurtling up the stairs.

'Duck!' thwucked the twins as they rocketed through the window yawning open at the top of the landing.

Nelly's cheeks began to flap and her stomach dropped like a stone. No sooner had they climbed the stairs than they were hurtling downwards towards the lawn and the open lounge windows.

'Hi, Mum and Dad!' squealed Bog and Blotch again as they rocketed past the fireplace, whistled past the sofa and spiralled out into the darkness of the back garden once more.

Nelly raised her arms above her head again and braced herself for a loop-the-loop twice around the entire house!

'This is BRILLLIAANNNNT!' she shouted, the stars blurring and giddying around her as her eyes watered with the chill and the thrill.

'Tentacles down!' she cheered, dropping her arms in time for re-entry into the house through the upstairs bedroom window.

The blue and green stripes of Bog and Blotch's wallpaper strobed past them before another whistling U-turn sent them tobogganing back through a different bedroom and across the duvet of Lump and Poltis's triple bed.

Round the bedroom three times they thundered, before rocketing back out into the landing.

'Going up!' shouted the twins excitedly as they

powered upwards through the open loft hatch.

'This is bonkers!' laughed Nelly, tucking her arms by her sides as they burst through the attic and rocketed towards the roof.

'Ha HA HA!' squealed the Dendrilegs twins.

'Hee HEE HEE!' came the reply.

Nelly's eyes darted left and right as the Centi Claws' legs suddenly retracted into the sides of their carriage.

'What's happening now?' she gasped.

'Surprise Number THREE!' laughed the twins as the final segment of the Centi Claws powered through the window in the roof and rocketed up towards the stars.

Nelly's eyes darted up, down and all around. The Centi Claws was soaring! They were soaring! High above the Montelimar Estate, the Centi Claws' crimson and white snake of a body was weaving through the night sky! If only her friends could see her NOW!

Nelly's hands reached out to squeeze the Dendrilegs' knees. Never mind her friends! If only Asti could see her now!

The quilting on her Puffa jacket pressed against the safety bars as she strained to get an aerial view of the Montelimar Estate.

With a hee hee hee and a spiralling swerve, the Centi Claws obliged with a steep, banking tilt.

'That's where the Muggots live!' Nelly shouted, pointing in the direction of the Badley Hall Estate. 'And the Cowcumbers live down there!' she said, turning as best she could to get a backwards view of Parma Drive. 'And way over there are the Altigators!' she cheered. 'And just over there are the Thermitts!'

'We know,' giggled Blotch.

'You've told us about the Thermitts before!' chuckled Bog.

Nelly turned excitedly towards the snaking line of the old Brown Canal to see if the Water Greeps' canal boat was visible. But before she could point a finger at the quietly bobbing lights, her chin dropped through her socks.

The Centi Claws was plummeting. And plummeting fast.

'Where are we going?' she asked.

'To find you some snow!' laughed the twins.

'Snow?' gasped Nelly.

'At the Thermitts'!' laughed Blotch. 'Dad phoned them earlier to see if it would be OK!'

'Surprise Number Four!' laughed Bog.

13

Humbug Crescent was approaching fast. Nelly could see the shape of the crescent. She could see the ice rink at the back of the Thermitts' house, and she could see Ig, Loo and Nippy waving to her from the open windows of their sub-zero home.

'It snows all winter round at the Thermitts'!' laughed Blotch. 'Didn't you know that?'

Nelly didn't know that. She knew it was cold but she didn't know that!

She was about to find out though.

A hundred metres ahead of them the gleaming head of the Centi Claws' snaking body was preparing to enter the Thermitts' open back door.

'Here we go again!' squealed Nelly as the legs attached to their carriage lowered into a landing position.

'Happy Christmas, Ig, Loo and Nippeeeeeeeeee!'

Segment by segment, leg by leg, the long snaking body that stretched before them entered the back door of the Thermitts' house.

'Prepare for entry!' shouted Nelly.

'Prepare for snowballs!' laughed Blotch.

'Here we goooooo!!!' whooped Bog.

The three friends braced themselves for a high-speed re-entry as the tail section of the Centi Claws powered closer and closer to the Thermitts' back garden.

'I've played with those curling stones!' Nelly pointed out as they rocketed over the back step.

With a shuddering jolt, Blotch, Bog and Nelly tobogganed straight through the brightly lit door frame and lurched hard right into the Arctic-white kitchen.

'Hard left next!' shouted Nelly, trying to give the twins some warning as to which way their big dipper was going to dip.

Bog and Blotch braced themselves but there was no need. Nelly had got it wrong. Instead of a left turn, there was a no-turn, followed by another jolt and a shudder.

Nelly and the two Dendrilegs slid forward into their safety bars as the carriage they were in unexpectedly slowed down.

'He's put the brakes on!' laughed Nelly.

She was right. The instant they had entered the sub-zero dining room the tail end of the Centi Claws had obligingly slowed. Its spiky red legs had lowered the entire length of its body and were now crawling at a snail's pace across carpets of deep snow.

Nelly and the twins caught their breath and looked around. The interior of the Thermitts' house was a winter wonderland. Snowflakes were falling like cotton wool balls from the ceiling above them and deep white snowdrifts were banking high against the walls.

'FUNTIME!' clapped Nelly. 'The Centi Claws is letting us play!'

'We thought you'd be pleased!' grinned the Dendrilegs.

Nelly leaned forward as much as the safety bars

would permit and scooped some snow up from around her knees.

'This is how you make a snowball!' she laughed, cupping two fistfuls of snow together and then moulding it into a ball.

'No, this is how you make a snowball, Nelly!' laughed Ig, bobbing her big blubbery Thermitt head up from behind an iceblock dining table.

Before Nelly could react, Ig let rip with a giant snowball of her own.

It was a Christmas ambush!

Nelly tried to dive for cover but the safety bars had her pinned just where the Thermitts wanted her.

'Use all your tentacles to throw with!' whooped Nelly. 'Let Snow Wars commence!'

With wide goofy grins, Blotch and Bog plunged their tentacles into the snowdrift that had collected in the carriage around their feet.

'This is how you make a snowball too!' laughed a second Thermitt, bobbing up from his hiding place behind the armchair in the lounge and launching a spectacularly accurate snowball directly into Nelly's open mouth.

Nelly spluttered the snow from her teeth and hurled a rather rushed snowball back. It broke up in mid-air and fell like talcum powder on to the armchair.

'Missed!' laughed Loo, bobbing down out of sight again and then reappearing with six more snowballs ready to go.

'That's cheating!' laughed Nelly, trundling like a fairground target slowly past the sofa. She and the twins were sitting ducks.

Nelly scooped some more snow into her hands and began pressing it firmly into a ball.

'We've made some more!' thwucked Blotch, tapping Nelly on the shoulder with a tentacle and then pointing to a huge pile of snowballs that were stacked up like a tray of Ferrero Rocher chocolates.

'Blimey!' laughed Nelly. 'Your tentacles made light work of that! Now then, where is little Nippy?' she murmured. 'I know he's hiding somewhere!'

'Here I am!' squeaked a voice from under the ice cube sofa cushions.

Nelly wheeled round to find the Thermitts' two-year-old son leaping from the sofa with a snowball in each paw. With a squeak of excitement he hurled both snowballs at once and then skied away on his long ski-length feet.

It was time to retaliate!

'FIRRRRRRE!' shouted Nelly, hurling her

snowball towards the sofa but hitting the wall thermostat instead.

Bog and Blotch grabbed tentacles full of snowballs from their pile and machine-gunned the room in all directions. Snowballs exploded from the white plastic wall, sending showers of snow down the backs of the sofa and chairs.

The Thermitts came out from their hiding places, snowballs blazing.

'Got you!' laughed Nelly, landing a snowball on Ig's second and third chins.

'Got YOU BOTH!' laughed Loo, skiing round behind them and slapping a snowball on each of the Dendrilegs' heads.

Bog and Blotch winced and then set about making some more reinforcements.

'It's not fair!' laughed Nelly, still pinned into position by the safety bars and trundling slightly quicker now in the direction of the hallway door. 'We can't move but you can ski all around the room!'

She was right, it wasn't fair. But it was FUN!

Fingers and tentacles cupped, pressed, patted

and threw. Snowballs missed, snowballs hit, snowballs crumbled, grenaded and flew.

'Yuk!' laughed Bog as he shook a third direct hit from his ear.

'Whoo-er!' said Nelly as she lurched back into her seat.

'Are you hit?' laughed Bog.

'No, we're moving!' smiled Nelly.

The elongated feet of the three Thermitts skied to a halt as the spiky red legs of the tail section lifted from the snow. The Centi Claws' body was picking up speed again and Nelly and the twins were leaving the room.

Nelly, Bog and Blotch unleashed their last snowballs with a chuckle and a wave and then braced themselves for a hard right turn.

Through the lounge door and into the hallway the Centi Claws' body snaked.

'Cool staircase!' laughed Blotch as they rocketed past the chairlifts at the bottom of the Thermitts' ice slope staircase.

'I've never seen up here before!' shouted Nelly as they powered on to the landing.

There was little to see, just a blur of white walls and a flash of white rooms, as the Centi Claws snaked, twisted and turned through the open doors and windows of the Thermitts' house before soaring back into the starry night sky.

'How fast was that?' gasped Nelly, swallowing a throatful of icy night air.

'We just switched to Centi Speed,' grinned Blotch.

It was Centi Speed all the way home for Nelly. At 9.30 precisely, the Centi Claws' landing gear touched down in the middle of a deserted Sweet Street.

The safety bars released their hold on Nelly's shoulders, and the Dendrilegs released their hold on Nelly's knees.

'Thank you so much!' said Nelly, kissing Bog and Blotch on the cheek. 'This has been totally the best Christmas Day ever!'

'You liked our surprises then!' thwucked Bog.

'I loved your surprises!' laughed Nelly, climbing out of her seat.

The red antennae lights switched brightly back

to green as a pair of coal-black eyes at the front twinkled a farewell.

'HEE HEE HEE,' whispered the Centi Claws.

Nelly raised a closed fist and waved.

'Goodbye!' she mouthed silently, for fear of bringing a neighbour to the window. 'See you again next year, perhaps!'

She turned to say a final goodbye to Bog and Blotch, but like a streak of red and white striped toothpaste the Centi Claws switched to Centi Speed again and was gone.

With her heart racing and her mind jangling, Nelly skipped up the path to her house.

Unusually, she didn't head straight for the lounge to share her adventures with her mum and dad. Instead she raced up the stairs to pay a visit to her sister.

'MUMMM!' came the unmistakable wail of Asti, screaming down the stairs. 'Nelly just hit me in the face with a snowball!'

'Don't be ridiculous,' burped her dad.

'Snowball indeed!' munched her mum.

'HEE HEE HEE!' chuckled Nelly.

Have you read the other
Nelly the Monster Sitter adventures?

When Petronella Morton puts an ad in the local newspaper
saying 'MONSTER SITTING AFTER SCHOOL AND
WEEKENDS. CALL NELLY,' little does she know that her
phone will begin to ring. AND RING AND RING AND RING.

Nelly soon discovers that there are families
of monsters living secretly all over the Montelimar Estate. Join
her at three addresses for three monstrously different baby
sitting adventures.

Hodder
Children's
Books

A division of Hachette Children's Books

Have you read the other
Nelly the Monster Sitter adventures?

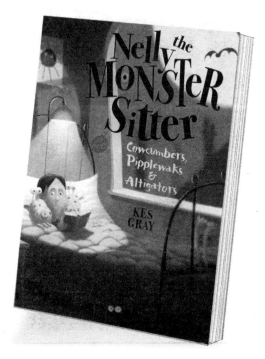

Nelly's phone is still ringing with lots more
monster sitting requests – and each one is
full of strange surprises including
weirdscreen TV trouble at number 11,
cracking excitement with the Pipplewaks
at number 66 and high rise hoodlum
hijinks with the Altigators at Eclair Towers.

Hodder
Children's
Books

A division of Hachette Children's Books

Have you read the other
Nelly the Monster Sitter adventures?

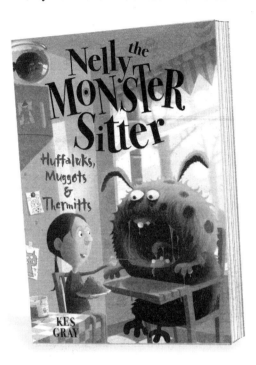

Nelly is as busy as ever looking after the
monster babies in her area. With each new
job Nelly never knows who or what is waiting
for her behind the door.
But one thing she can be sure of -
monster sitting is never dull!

Hodder
Children's
Books

A division of Hachette Children's Books

Have you read the other
Nelly the Monster Sitter adventures?

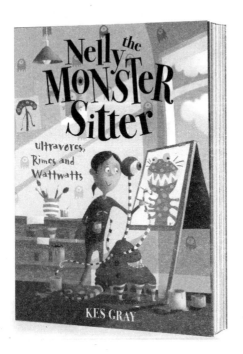

Things are getting stickier and stickier
for Nelly. Undone by flies at the Ultravores,
lost for words at the Rimes,
plus the shock of her life at the Wattwatts!

Hodder
Children's
Books

A division of Hachette Children's Books